MW01094614

Praise for BECOMING MUHAMMAD ALI

"Cassius Clay's kinetic boyhood—depicted through prose, poetry, and illustration—is the prism through which this uplifting novel casts the myth of the legendary boxer."
—*New York Times*, **Best Children's Books of the Year**

"This utterly delightful story about Ali's childhood is a smash hit. Get this uplifting, informative book onto library shelves and into kids' hands."
—*School Library Journal*, **starred review**

"Patterson and Alexander, two heavyweights in the world of books, unite to tell the story of how Cassius Clay grew up to be Muhammad Ali, one of the greatest boxers of all time."
—*The Horn Book*, **starred review**

"The prose and poems reflect Clay's public bravado and private humbleness as well as his appreciation and respect for family and friends. A knockout!"
—*Booklist*, **starred review**

"Spare...witty...Cassius's narrative illustrates his charisma [and] drive...Powerful, accessible view of a fascinating figure."
—*Publishers Weekly*, **starred review**

"A stellar collaboration that introduces an important and intriguing individual to today's readers."
—*Kirkus Reviews*, **starred review**

"These lightning-bolt figures are poetry surrounded by prose...a kinetic, dazzling experience...Like the world many adolescents inhabit, the world that *Becoming Muhammad Ali* presents is complex...But most importantly, it's a reminder that once upon a time Cassius Clay, all poetry and italics, was a kid like the rest of us. It is my hope that Black children read this book, see themselves in young Clay, and know that they too are poetry made flesh."
—*New York Times Book Review*

Praise for the MAXIMUM RIDE Series

School's Out—Forever

"Readers are in for another exciting, wild ride."
—**Kirkus Reviews**

Praise for the MIDDLE SCHOOL Series

Middle School, The Worst Years of My Life

"A keen appreciation of kids' insecurities and an even more astute understanding of what might propel boy readers through a book...a perfectly pitched novel."
—**Los Angeles Times**

"Cleverly delves into the events that make middle school so awkward: cranky bus drivers, tardy slips, bathroom passes, and lots of rules."
—**Associated Press**

Praise for the JACKY HA-HA Series

Jacky Ha-Ha

"A strong female protagonist, realistic characters, and a balanced approach to middle-school life make this book a winner."
—**Common Sense Media**

"James Patterson has figured out the formula for writing entertaining books for tween readers."
—**Parents' Choice**

JIMMY PATTERSON BOOKS FOR YOUNG READERS BY JAMES PATTERSON

Ali Cross

Ali Cross
Ali Cross: Like Father, Like Son

Daniel X

The Dangerous Days of Daniel X
Daniel X: Watch the Skies
Daniel X: Demons and Druids
Daniel X: Game Over
Daniel X: Armageddon
Daniel X: Lights Out

Dog Diaries

Dog Diaries
Dog Diaries: Happy Howlidays
Dog Diaries: Mission Impawsible
Dog Diaries: Curse of the Mystery Mutt
Dog Diaries: Ruffing It
Dog Diaries: Dinosaur Disaster

House of Robots

House of Robots
House of Robots: Robots Go Wild!
House of Robots: Robot Revolution

I Funny

I Funny
I Even Funnier
I Totally Funniest
I Funny TV
I Funny: School of Laughs
The Nerdiest, Wimpiest, Dorkiest I Funny Ever

Jacky Ha-Ha

Jacky Ha-Ha
Jacky Ha-Ha: My Life Is a Joke
Jacky Ha-Ha: A Graphic Novel
Jacky Ha-Ha: My Life Is a Joke (A Graphic Novel)

Katt vs. Dogg

Katt vs. Dogg
Katt Loves Dogg

Max Einstein

Max Einstein: The Genius Experiment
Max Einstein: Rebels with a Cause
Max Einstein Saves the Future
World Champions! A Max Einstein Adventure

Middle School

Middle School, The Worst Years of My Life
Middle School: Get Me out of Here!
Middle School: Big Fat Liar
Middle School: How I Survived Bullies, Broccoli, and Snake Hill
Middle School: Ultimate Showdown
Middle School: Save Rafe!
Middle School: Just My Rotten Luck
Middle School: Dog's Best Friend
Middle School: Escape to Australia
Middle School: From Hero to Zero
Middle School: Born to Rock
Middle School: Master of Disaster
Middle School: Field Trip Fiasco
Middle School: It's a Zoo in Here

Treasure Hunters

Treasure Hunters
Treasure Hunters: Danger Down the Nile
Treasure Hunters: Secret of the Forbidden City
Treasure Hunters: Peril at the Top of the World
Treasure Hunters: Quest for the City of Gold
Treasure Hunters: All-American Adventure
Treasure Hunters: The Plunder Down Under

Becoming Muhammad Ali (cowritten with Kwame Alexander)

Best Nerds Forever

Laugh Out Loud

Not So Normal Norbert

Pottymouth and Stoopid

Public School Superhero

Scaredy Cat

Unbelievably Boring Bart

Word of Mouse

For exclusives, trailers, and other information, visit jimmypatterson.org.

JAMES PATTERSON
and CHRIS GRABENSTEIN

Illustrated by Anuki López

JIMMY Patterson Books
Little, Brown and Company
New York Boston London

Copyright © 2021 by James Patterson
Illustrations by Anuki López

Cover art © Lisa Manuzak Wiley. Cover lettering by Jennet Liaw.
Cover copyright © 2021 by Hachette Book Group, Inc.

JIMMY Patterson Books / Little, Brown and Company
Hachette Book Group
1290 Avenue of the Americas, New York, NY 10104
JimmyPatterson.org

First Edition: December 2021

JIMMY Patterson Books is an imprint of Little, Brown and Company, a division of Hachette Book Group, Inc. The Little, Brown name and logo are trademarks of Hachette Book Group, Inc. The JIMMY Patterson Books® name and logo are trademarks of JBP Business, LLC.

The publisher is not responsible for websites (or their content) that are not owned by the publisher.

Library of Congress Control Number: 2021945374

ISBNs: 978-0-316-50017-3 (hardcover), 978-0-316-50065-4 (ebook)

Printed in the United States of America

LSC-H

Printing 1, 2021

Chapter 1

Oscar leapt up, grabbed the hawk, yanked it down, and thrashed it all around.

It was his favorite thing to do—especially since the rubber hawk had a noisy squeaker that honked and tooted inside its belly.

Next, Oscar pretended to swim across a raging river and dodge a weaselboar—a snarling beast that was half weasel and half boar and not something most doggs could dodge the way Oscar could dodge it, even if this weaselboar was made out of stuffed pillowcases and had the tip of a tin funnel for its pointy tusk.

Pretending to make exciting action-adventure moves was his other favorite thing.

Now he chased after a flying squirrel zipping across the stage on a cable.

Chasing squirrels—real, fake, or in-between— was probably his favorite *favorite* thing.

His friend Molly stood on the other side of the stage, dramatically, describing every move Oscar made.

"Oscar saved me from the clawing, clasping clutches of a horrible, hovering hawk. When a wild weaselboar attacked us on the edge of a cliff, Oscar heroically protected me and dodged to the side—sending that weaselboar on a one-way trip to the valley below. He also laughed in the face of danger *and* the face of a mountain lion! When he was injured, I nursed him back to health with medicinal herbs and my comforting, well-enunciated words."

Molly was an actress. She described everything dramatically.

She was also a katt.

Hanging out with Molly the katt? It was Oscar's new favorite thing to do, even though his mother, father, sister, cousins, neighbors, and even his dogg groomer all thought it was kind of weird. For years, katts and doggs had been sworn enemies. But then Oscar and Molly both got lost in the woods. At the same time! The only way to survive was to help each other. Now they were best friends forever.

"Finally," gushed Molly, stepping into the spotlight while Oscar strode across the stage riding a make-believe moose on a stick, "after many long days and many longer nights filled with danger and darkness—because, hello, it was night—we made it back to civilization! All of Kattsburgh and all of Doggsylvania rejoiced! Katts and doggs all over this great land came out of their dogg houses and their katt condos to march in Welcome Home Molly and Oscar parades where they held paws and sang 'Kumbaya' together in perfect harmony!"

It was time for Oscar's big line. "For, in the end, we are all stronger when we work together. Because katts are, basically, the same as doggs!" And then he ad-libbed a little. "Except the whole litter box thing. I still don't get that. Why would anybody want to spend all that time burying their poop when they could just drop and go?"

Molly gave him a look. It was the same look she gave him every time he veered off the script from the show they put on twice a week for tourists at the Western Frontier Park's welcome center.

Oscar smiled at the audience sheepishly. "Um,

forget that part about the poop, please. Thank you."

"We hope none of you get lost in the park," said Molly, wrapping things up. "But if you do, remember: we're all in this together!"

She threw up her arms and basked in the spotlight, waiting for the audience to clap and cheer and shout, "Brava!"

But they didn't. Except the seal in the front row. (They'll flap their flippers for anything.)

Unfortunately, the doggs in the auditorium were snarling and the katts were grumbling.

Oscar's tail drooped between his legs when he heard the sour reaction.

Because he knew what was coming next.

The questions! Oh, how he hated the questions.

Chapter 2

Molly fluffed up her snowy white fur and twinkled her sky-blue eyes.

She was an actress. She could act like she wasn't afraid of what she knew would come next.

She decided to pick the clapping seal in the front row for the first question after the show.

"Yes?" she purred. "The seal in the front row. Do you have a question?"

"Yup, yup," said the blubbery seal, slapping his slippery flippers together. "I do. I sure do. Uhhhh. Where's the bathroom?"

Molly gave the seal a withering look. But of course Oscar (ever the Dogg Scout) wagged his tail cheerfully.

"Oh, I know that one," he said. "It's outside. Anywhere outside. The bathroom is just, you know, *outside*."

"Thanks!" barked the seal as he quickly waddled out of the auditorium.

Now there was nobody in the audience except katts, doggs, and a pair of hungry raccoons who were both rummaging for snacks upside down in the garbage cans at the back of the auditorium.

Several angry paws shot up.

"Um, okay," said Molly. "Since nobody has any questions…"

"Sure they do, Molly," said Oscar, trying to be helpful. "See all those raised paws? That means they all have questions even though we don't really want to answer them after what happened during our last Q and A, but, well, if you announce that there's going to be a question and answer session, you really have to take questions and answers. Well, you only *take* the questions. You *give* the answers. You could also just answer the questions. That'd work, too."

Molly rolled her eyes. Her wilderness survival partner was babbling. Oscar babbled a lot when he was nervous. He probably even had a Dogg Scout merit badge in babbling.

"I got a question, little kitty," snarled a dogg with floppy jowls. Stringy white drool was dangling from both corners of his mouth. "Who says doggs and katts have to dwell together in peas and harmonicas?"

Molly fluttered her whiskers. "Um, that's not what we said…"

The dogg ignored her. "I don't want to be sitting in a pile of peas with a bunch of dang katts blowing on a harmonica. When I come to the Western Frontier Park, I want a katt-free campground and a doggs-only dining hall. Like we had back in the good old days before you two got all lost and helped each other and all that other malarkey I'm sick and tired of hearing about on TV."

"It's peace and harmony, sir," Molly explained as sweetly as she could. "Peace and harmony."

"Ah, bully sticks. That's even worse!"

"I'll say," sniffed a snooty Persian katt. "Why must we share our family vacation with these...these...doggs? They're all so frightfully uncouth—forever sniffing each other's derrieres and chasing after anything tossed their way."

The dogg snarled. "Well, at least we doggs don't do lick-yourself-yoga all day every day like you feline fur balls!"

"Kindly turn your head when you bellow, you brutish beast," said the katt, crinkling his nose. "I'm afraid you have a permanent case of dogg breath."

"Ah, why don't you go hock up a hair ball!"

"And why don't you go get a rabies shot! In your butt!"

Soon all the doggs and all the katts in the auditorium were snapping and sniping and hissing and hooting and yipping and yapping at one another.

"Enough!" shrieked a commanding voice.

It was Molly and Oscar's boss.

The head park ranger.

The majestic hawkowl!

Chapter 3

Oscar remembered back to the first time he ever saw the hawkowl.

He'd thought she was weird. And freaky. Freaky weird.

Half hawk, half owl, she was one of the many mythical (some would say magical) creatures that lived in the Western Frontier Park. She was also in charge of the whole park, including the shows Oscar and Molly put on in the welcome center.

"Rules are rules," she proclaimed. "Here in the

park, we must all learn to live together in peace and harmony."

"Again with the peas and harmonica," muttered the dogg, who never really paid attention to what anybody else said.

"Therefore," the noble hawkowl continued, "as we have all learned from Molly and Oscar during their informative and instructional welcoming presentation, inside the borders of the Western Frontier Park you must get along with your fellow, if historically different, creatures. Or you may choose to spend your vacation somewhere else."

That quieted the room.

For maybe five seconds.

"Fine," growled the jowly dogg. "I hear they're still doing it old-school over in the Eastern Wilderness Reserve. Separate dogg and katt accommodations."

"Nyes," purred the Persian. "I must admit I have heard the same thing. There's a katt zone and a dogg zone. And you can definitely smell when you've reached the border."

"Yeah," snapped the dogg, "because it stinks like katt pee!"

"More like wet dogg."

"Katt pee!"

"Wet dogg!"

"Guards?" shouted the hawkowl, flapping her wings. "Security?"

Three ferocious-looking grizzly wolves—half bear, half wolf, and all muscle—marched into the room.

And then they marched the katts and doggs out of the auditorium.

All except Molly and Oscar.

"We need to talk," said the hawkowl after the auditorium had been cleared. "I'm afraid I have some bad news."

"Somebody claimed those shoes I chewed?" said Oscar. "Because I swear I found them in the trash bin…"

The hawkowl shook her wise head. "No, Oscar. We're going to have to let you two go. There will be no more welcome shows."

Molly gasped. "No more shows? But the show must go on! Everybody in showbiz knows that."

"Not if nobody wants to see the show," said the hawkowl with a sigh so heavy it ruffled her neck feathers. "In fact, it seems not many doggs or katts want to even visit the Western Frontier Park ever since we ended the strict segregation of species and started our policy of mixing and mingling."

"Speaking of mixing and mingling," said Molly, "Oscar and I were supposed to be the queen and king of the first-ever All Animals Ball."

"I like balls," said Oscar. "The slimier and squeakier the better!"

"The ball—a fancy dance, in this instance—will most likely be canceled," said the hawkowl. "I'm afraid, as you once again witnessed, the world of 'sworn enemies' has not really changed."

"It has for us!" insisted Oscar.

"It's true," said Molly. "Oscar and I both learned we're better together."

"I'm afraid you two are in the minority," sighed the hawkowl. "More doggs and katts are spending their vacations at the Eastern Wilderness Reserve, where 'Doggs Can Be Doggs and Katts Can Be Katts.' But, my young friends, like you I refuse to give up all hope. In the end, maybe when you two are the grown-ups, the fighting will end and the world will be a better place. But it's going to take time, children. Lots and lots of time."

Chapter 4

Molly had a sad expression on her face when she and Oscar exited the welcome center for what would probably be the very last time.

Then she switched to her annoyed face. And her angry face. She even did "confused." She was an *actress*! Therefore, unlike most katts, she had to be able to display a wide range of emotions, not just "bored" or "hissy." She longed to one day be a megastar like Fleas Witherspoon or Meowncé.

"Want me to run you home on my back?"

asked Oscar. He was a very good runner. When they were lost in the wilderness, he saved Molly a few times by letting her ride or cross a stream on his back. In return, she scratched the part of his neck he never could reach, no matter how many pretzel twist contortions he made. They were a good team. Working together had saved their lives.

It was too bad that most of the doggs and katts in Kattsburgh and Doggsylvania refused to follow in their paw prints.

"I can't," said Molly, gesturing toward a big SUV that had just pulled into the gravel driveway. "Unfortunately, my parents are here to pick me up." She sighed dramatically. "Guess I'll have to tell them the news. Like so many actors, I am now…" She put the back of her paw to her forehead. "Unemployed."

"Oh, hey!" said Oscar, tail wagging. "Here come my folks, too!"

A rusty, banged-up pickup truck rumbled to a stop behind the katts' SUV as its driver's-side tinted window lowered. Molly's father, Boomer Hissleton the Third, Esquire, stuck out his head. "Molly, darling? Are you ready to skedaddle?" Mr. Hissleton was giving Oscar a snooty look.

"Yes, Daddy," said Molly.

"Well scamper along, then, dear. We have reservations at Chez Kattnip. It's Two-for-One Tuna Tuesday."

Molly turned to Oscar. "See you…whenever. I hope we can still do stuff together."

"Yeah," said Oscar. "Me, too. But I don't think our parents are going to let us, even though they should." Oscar's tail sagged as he realized that this might be the last time he ever saw his katt friend. If everybody was going back to the old ways, his parents might make him chase her up a tree the next time he saw her.

"So long, Molly. It's been, you know, fun. Lots and lots of fun."

Molly nodded. "Maybe the hawkowl is right. Maybe when we're the grown-ups, the world will be as good as we know it could be."

"Yeah. I'd like that."

Molly bit her lip and scurried off to climb into her family's waiting SUV.

"Take forever, why don't you," said her brother, Blade, as Molly buckled into her seat. As usual, Blade's eyes were glued to the screen of his video game gizmo. Electronic *boop-boop-bloop* music played as he chased tiny pixelated mice around a maze. "This game is too much work," he whined. "I like the one with the red dot better."

"Wake me up when we get there, Boomer," purred Molly's mother. She was curled up in the sunny front seat, napping. "And take the route with the most sunbeams."

"Of course, Fluffy, darling," said Molly's father with a yawn. "I could go for a kattnap myself. I haven't had one for more than fifteen minutes."

"Daddy?" said Molly.

"Yes, dear?"

"One, you're driving. You can't nap."

"Point taken. And what's your number two?"

"I lost my job."

"Excuse me?"

"They don't want Oscar and me doing our welcome-to-the-park shows anymore. Apparently, certain katts and doggs don't want to hear our heroic story or share the park or even try to get along anymore."

"Is that so? Oh, dear. What a frightful shame. I'm so, so sorry to hear it."

The way he smirked and wiggled his eyebrows when he said that?

He wasn't sorry at all.

Chapter 5

As the dogg family's pickup truck rumbled toward the park exit, Oscar stared at the passing scenery and told his family the sad, sad news.

"Son?" said his father. "Is what you just told us the dadgum truth? There ain't gonna be no more of them sappy 'oh, watch how we saved each other' shows?"

"Nope. Sadly, this was our last day!"

"Woof-hoo!" howled his father as the truck passed under the park's rustic entry arch. "Good riddance to bad rubbish!"

"But Molly and I are friends!" Oscar protested, but his father didn't hear him because he'd jammed his paw down on the gas pedal and made the engine roar. The truck rocked up the road, chasing after Molly's SUV.

"Duke?" said Oscar's mother. "Why are you driving like a maniac?"

"Because I'm happy, Lola! Driving like a maniac is what I do when I'm happy!"

"Can't you just, like, wag your tail or something?" said Oscar's teenage sister, Fifi. "The way you're driving, all herky-jerky? I could so totally get carsick."

"Duke?" cried Oscar's mom. "You're scaring me and the children."

"Then sit on a wee-wee pad, Lola. You, too, Fifi. I need to pass that toffee-nosed tabby's SUV." Oscar's father put on his funny katt voice. "'Oooh. I'm Boomer Hissleton the Third, Esquire. I'm so fancy. I fart rainbows.'"

"Fa-ther?" said Fifi. "I'm going to, like, puke a Technicolor rainbow if you don't slow down! I get carsick."

"Well, darlin', today's your lucky day."

The dogg truck passed the katt SUV.

"Just roll down your window and let 'er rip. It's payback time. Remember when Molly's stupid brother Blade hocked up that hair ball and splattered it all over our windshield? Never could scrape away all that chunky crud."

"Um, Dad?" said Oscar, hanging on to an overhead handle as the rickety truck rocketed up the road. "That was a long time ago."

"So? A dogg never forgets!"

"You're thinking about elephants, dear," shrieked Oscar's mother.

"Huh? Oh, never mind. I forgot what we were talking about. One thing I do remember? We hate katts but we hate Hissletons even more!"

"We do?" said Oscar, sounding surprised. "Why?"

"Because we do. Always have. Always will."

"But, why, Dad?"

"Aw, cheese and sausages. I forget that, too." Oscar's dad swerved the truck back and forth a few times.

Oscar's sister had her paw to her mouth and

her face fur was turning green. "Yurp," was all she could say.

"Honestly, Duke," said Oscar's mother, rolling her eyes. "When we get home, you need to take a distemper shot. Maybe two."

"All right, Fifi," Oscar's father shouted over his shoulder to his daughter. "Give them swanky katts a taste of their own hair balls!"

Fifi burped. Then she belched. Then her stomach settled down. "Sorry, Daddy. It was just gas. I don't need to hurl anymore."

"Well, hurl some insults at that Hissleton girl in the back seat."

"But that's Molly," Oscar protested.

"So?" said his dad, glaring up at him in the rearview mirror.

Oscar was torn. Molly was his friend. But his father was his father. Always had been. Always would be. Molly was just someone he'd met when he chased a flying squirrel and got lost in the wilderness. She wasn't family. Sure, she'd kind of, sort of saved his life but he'd saved hers, too.

They were even, right?

They didn't have to stay best friends forever, did they?

Fifi started barking at Molly (who'd made the mistake of rolling down her window so she could wave good-bye to Oscar).

"You're so ugly," Fifi shouted, "when your parents drop you off at school, I bet they have to pay a fine for littering!"

Oscar's father laughed. His mother chuckled.

Oscar? He just sank down in his seat and tried not to whimper.

Chapter 6

Good dogg!" Oscar's dad told Fifi as she kept spewing insults at Molly. "Such a good, good dogg!"

"Thanks, Daddy," said Fifi, her tail happily thumping the seat.

Oscar cringed and closed his eyes.

"Help your sister, Oscar," urged his father. "Tell Molly you know she's afraid of trees—because of their bark!"

Fortunately, the two cars reached a fork in the road. Molly and her family went left for

Kattsburgh. Oscar and his family went right for Doggsylvania. Oscar heaved a sigh of relief.

His dad was looking at him in the rearview mirror again. "Did you just heave a sigh of relief, son?"

"No, I'm just, you know, sulking. I didn't get to yell anything at the katts. I was going to, uh, tell Molly to go eat a mice cream cone."

"Why? Katts love mice cream!"

"What a totally dumb insult," huffed his sister. "You are such an embarrassment to this family, Oscar. I don't even know how we could be, like, related."

Oscar didn't say another word for the rest of the ride home.

When they pulled into the driveway of their split-level dogg house, Oscar's father screeched the truck to a stop so he could yank open the mailbox.

"Bills, bills, bills," he muttered. "*Dogg Gourmet* magazine."

"That's mine," said Oscar's mom. "I hope they have a new recipe for Chunky Lumpy Stew..."

Oscar's dad flipped through the stack of mail and found another magazine. "*Teen Dogg Beat.* That's yours, Fifi."

He tossed it into the back seat. When Fifi saw who was on the cover, she shrieked. "The Beagles! They are so awesome. 'I Want to Hold Your Paw' is the most awesome song ever!"

Oscar's father snorted. "You call those four howlers a band? They're just a bunch of shaggy-haired mutts." He flicked through the envelopes and came upon a letter. "It's for you, Oscar."

"Really?" Oscar couldn't think of anybody who might write him a letter. Except maybe Molly. She'd sent him a lot of thank-you notes after he, more or less, saved her life. "Who's it from?"

"Your cousin Romaldo."

"Cousin Romaldo?!?" said Fifi. "Cousin Romaldo is so super cool. I wish he were my brother…"

"Why's he writing to Oscar?" wondered his mother.

"Probably a Dogg Scout thing," said Oscar, reaching for the letter. "He might need a few pointers. I've heard that Cousin Romaldo is the worst Dogg Scout ever. He even flunked the test for his biscuits and bones merit badge."

His father gave Oscar the letter.

"Open it up!" said Fifi. "Let me read it."

Oscar was about to slit the envelope open with a flick of his claw when he noticed the stamp.

It contained a pretty lame and easy-to-decipher Dogg Scout mirror reverse code. Oscar quickly slid his paw over the stamp so no one else could read what was printed on it: a nonsense word spelled T-E-R-C-E-S, repeated four times. The first one was underlined. Because it was the top one.

The top TERCES.

Or, when you flipped it, the top SECRET!

Chapter 7

Oscar scampered into the house.

He wanted to be in his room before he opened the "top secret" letter from Cousin Romaldo.

"I want to read that letter," said Fifi, grabbing for the envelope.

"It's addressed to me," Oscar reminded her.

"So? What does that have to do with anything?"

Oscar snarled. Fifi snarled back.

"Children?" said their mother. "That's enough snarling for one day. Both of you—go to your rooms and finish your homework. We have company coming for dinner tonight. Your grandfather Max is driving up from Barkansas."

"Dagnabit. I forgot to pick up a bucket of fried chicken gizzards," said Oscar's father, spinning his truck keys around his paw. "You know how much my dad loves his Barkansas Fried Gizzards."

"Well, run to BFG," said Oscar's mother. "And Duke? Make sure you get extra gravy and dogg biscuits. The chunky kind."

"The gravy or the biscuits?"

"Both, Duke. Both."

"Yes, Lola."

His father went back out to the truck. Oscar ducked into his room and locked the door.

Why would Cousin Romaldo write to me? he wondered. *Why would he write a letter instead of texting?*

But then Oscar remembered. Romaldo was very...poetic. Marched to the beat of his own squeaky toy. He was also a teenager. Even older than Fifi. He lived on the other side of Doggsylvania, in a place called Fidodelphia. Oscar hadn't even seen Romaldo since a wedding his parents dragged him to. (It wasn't all bad. There was meatloaf cake with lard icing decorated with bacon bits.)

There was only one way for Oscar to find out what the letter was all about. He'd have to read it. He sliced open the envelope, unfolded the fancy paper, and read what his cousin had written:

Dear Cousin Oscar:

Thank you for all you have done to promote the power of LOVE. Love, as they say, is a many-splendored thing. It's the April rose that only grows in the early spring. The golden crown that makes a dogg a king, even if his name is Romaldo and not King. I, dear cousin, am in love.

The message was super syrupy sweet—like a puddle of melted Frosty Paws Ice Cream. In other words, it was pure Romaldo. Oscar thought he might hurl if he read any more of it, but a Dogg Scout is brave and courageous. So he read on…

And now to my real reason for writing you. I have fallen in love with a katt named Violet. Just like you fell in love with a katt named Molly in the wilderness and on that TV show. Oh, what a kiss you two shared! I need your help, Oscar. I am working on a plan to make sure Violet and I can live happily ever after. I would appreciate your input, since you know so much about dogg-katt relationships.

Sincerely yours,
and I mean that sincerely,
Cousin Romaldo

Now Oscar really thought he might lose his lunch all over the shag carpet. Romance? Between his goofy cousin Romaldo and a katt named Violet? This was sappier than the maple tree he'd peed on yesterday.

Romaldo, of course, was correct. Molly and Oscar *had* been on a TV show, right after they survived in the wilderness together. The Weasel

Broadcasting Network called it *Sworn Enemies for Life: Katt vs. Dogg* and, at the end of the show, Molly surprised Oscar with (yuck) a kiss. A real smoocharoo.

But no way were Oscar and Molly in love. That would just be gross.

"I don't need to see this mushy stuff!" he said

36

to himself, crumpling Romaldo's letter into a paper ball. "And I definitely don't want anybody else seeing it!"

He ate the balled-up letter.

It was so sweet, it gave him a stomachache.

Chapter 8

About an hour after Oscar swallowed Cousin Romaldo's letter, his dad started howling for Oscar and Fifi to come out of their rooms.

"Oscar? Fifi? Get your tails out here in the living room. Come sniff Grandpa Max's butt!"

Oscar rolled his eyes. Sniffing butts was how doggs said hello and every dogg you met had their own peculiar, personal scent. Doggs who sniffed Oscar's butt said he smelled like peanut butter. Grandpa Max? Oscar had only met him a few times, since he lived far away in Barkansas. But his odor was very bitter and extremely sour. Like pickles floating in a tub of vinegar and spoiled milk.

According to Oscar's dad, Grandpa Max was always angry about everything. He'd been that way even before his wife, Grandma Shirley, passed away. But once he became a widower, he was even worse.

"Where are my ungrateful grandchildren?" Oscar heard his grandpa growl. "Get out here and sniff my butt!"

"Hello, Grandpa Max," Oscar heard Fifi say on the other side of his bedroom door. She sounded terrified.

"You call that a collar?" grumbled the old dogg. "Go put on something without all those rhinestones, young lady!"

"Yes, Grandpa."

Oscar took a deep breath and wished he were a greyhound. Sure, he could run twenty-seven miles per hour. But greyhounds? They could run forty-four. And that's what Grandpa Max always made Oscar want to do. Run away! Fast! Instead, he shuffled into the hallway with his tail tucked between his legs and his eyes glued to the floor.

"Um, hello, Grandpa Max."

"There he is," said Oscar's grandfather, curling up one side of his snout to show Oscar a few very brown teeth. "The boy who disgraced our entire family by helping a katt. And not just any katt. Oh, no. It had to be a Hissleton. Little Molly Hissleton. We hate the Hissletons, boy! Always have, always will."

Oscar dared to raise his eyes. "We do? Why?"

"Because I said so!"

"Pappy?" said Oscar's father. "The boy's ignorance of that particular family tradition of hatin' the Hissletons is partly my fault."

"What? He inherited your dumb?"

"No. I forgot to tell Oscar and Fifi about our family feud. In fact, I plumb forgot about the feud, too."

"What?" snapped Grandpa Max. "How could you?"

"Well, my memory's not so good, Pappy. I sometimes wish I were an elephant."

"What?!?"

"Lola tells me elephants never forget nothin'. 'Course, they also eat a lot of peanuts and I've got me that nut allergy..."

Grandpa Max shook his head. "This is exactly why I drove up this way. We're all going to the Eastern Wilderness Reserve for a family reunion."

"We are?" said Fifi. "Aren't there, like, mosquitos and fleas and ticks?"

"Yes! We're going to ruff it. You. Your disappointing little brother. Your father, your mother, your aunts, your uncles, your cousins—the whole Montahugh clan. It's time you all started remembering who we are and what we stand for. We're going on a wilderness retreat to reconnect with our roots."

"Oh, boy," said Oscar, wagging his tail slightly. "Are we going to chomp on tree branches? Because I know a golden retriever, her name is Goldie, and Goldie's always dragging around a tree branch and—"

"No, you floppy-eared idiot," sneered Grandpa Max. "We're not going into the wilderness to play with the trees. We're going there to reconnect with our basic instincts. Our doggliness."

Fifi raised her paw.

"What?" barked Grandpa Max.

"Will Cousin Romaldo be coming on this family reunion camping trip?"

"Yes! And it's not a camping trip. It's a wilderness adventure!"

"Fur sure," said Fifi. "But if Romaldo's going to be there, I need to pack some extra grooming products."

"Later, Fifi," said Oscar's dad. "Right now, we need to eat our extra crispy, extra greasy gizzards. They're Grandpa's favorite, right, Pappy?"

"Shuddup, son! I'm getting hangry!"

"Then let's eat!" said Oscar's mother cheerfully.

Oscar slumped his shoulders and slouched into the dining room with his family.

His family, the Montahughs, hated Molly's family, the Hissletons.

That was horrible.

And right now, Oscar sort of wished he belonged to some other family. One without Grandpa Max.

Chapter 9

Later that night, at Molly Hissleton's home in Kattsburgh, the whole family was gathered in the den watching the newest hit on the Weasel Broadcasting Network: *Furry Family Feud,* a game show starring the same ferret who'd hosted Molly and Oscar's "Katt vs. Dogg" event.

"Hello, ladies, gentlemen, llamas, and gerbils," said the ferret through her nose. "Thank you so much for joining us for this evening's *Furry Family Feud.* Trust me, folks. The fur is about to fly. Big time."

"Oh, my," said Molly's father. "Is that a family of seals? They don't have fur, do they?"

"A little bit," said Blade, who'd done a report on seals for school. "But mostly they use their blubber to stay warm."

"Nyes," said Molly's father, contentedly rubbing his belly. "I do much the same thing."

Molly was having a hard time focusing on the TV game show. Her mind kept spinning back to that dogg-awful car ride home and the horrible things Oscar's sister yelled at her. Molly remembered telling Oscar that they would be BFFs—Best Friends Forever. She figured that's what happened after you saved each other's lives on a daily basis. And now? Oscar let his big sister say mean things about Molly!

She was only half listening when the ferret introduced the family of seals. One was in the navy. One ran a Christmas shop. Another did something in the legal field.

"Oh, dudes!" said Blade, who seldom got excited about anything. "This is going to be sooooo awesome. The other family is a bunch of polar bears!

Seals and polar bears? Prey and predator. Total natural enemies to the max."

"Do we have to watch this?" asked Molly with a sigh.

"Hmmm?" said her mother, who was napping on the couch.

"Do. We. Have. To. Watch. This!"

"Nyes, Molly," said her father. "Blade and I find it fascinating. It appeals to our keenly honed hunting instincts."

"Totally," said Blade, who, for the first time since forever, wasn't glued to his game gizmo. "The ferret was totally correct. The fur is about to fly fur sure."

"Turn that fool thing off!" commanded the very domineering voice of an elderly and imperious katt who had just strode into the room.

"Mother dear?" said Molly's father, pawing the remote to snap off the TV.

"Hey!" cried Blade as the screen went black. "We were watching that!"

"And now, you are not," proclaimed Molly and Blade's grandmother, Theodosia Hissleton. She had inherited her husband's entire fortune when he passed away and was now the wealthiest katt in all of Kattsburgh.

I'm so rich, I buy a new yacht every time the old one gets wet.

"Grandmama?" said Molly, fluttering her eyelashes daintily, the way she knew her grandmother liked for her to flutter them.

"Hello, Molly, darling. Blade? Get your paws off the furniture! You weren't raised in a barn!"

"Yes, Grandmama," mumbled Blade.

"Whatever brings you to our humble abode, Mother darling?" asked Molly's father.

"Is someone here?" asked Molly's mother, stretching into a yawn.

"Yes, Fluffy. Time to wakey, wakey. 'Tis I. Theodosia. The matriarch of the Hissleton family!"

"Um, what's a matriarch?" asked Blade.

"The woman in charge," said Theodosia. "The queen."

"Oh. Cool."

"Boomer?"

"Yes, mother of mine?"

"We have a situation."

"Oh, dear. How may we be of assistance?"

"By helping me knock some sense into your niece, Violet!"

"Cousin Violet?" gasped Molly. "She's so elegant and glamorous."

"Hmmpfh," huffed Grandmama. "Not anymore. Her parents tell me she has fallen in love with... with..."

"With who?" asked Molly's mother.

Theodosia Hissleton closed her eyes as she summoned up the strength to answer the question.

"An alley katt! There. I said it. Her parents are at their wits' end. They don't know what to do. Violet intends to run off with a flea-bitten, fur-matted, scurvy scoundrel of a katt named Tom. This Tom spends his nights sitting on top of dented garbage can lids yowling at the moon!"

"Cool," said Blade.

His grandmother gave him an icy stare. "No, Blade. It is not 'cool.' It is disgraceful. And it must be stopped!"

Chapter 10

An alley katt?" sniffed Molly's father. "How absolutely horrid."

"And his name is Tom?" asked Molly's mother. "Tom Katt? Are you sure that isn't an alias? A nom de guerre?"

"It does not matter whether the rascal's name is Tom, Simba, or Oreo. We must put an end to this romance. Immediately!" said Theodosia.

"But how?" asked Molly's father. "Has her father, my beloved brother Mister Cookiepants, had a word with her?"

"Several," said Theodosia. "And her mother, Fuzzybutt, also tried to talk some sense into the girl. Alas, it was of no avail. There is nothing more they can do. You know how stubborn teenage girls can be."

"Not yet," said Molly's mother. "Our Molly is still such an angel."

Molly smiled modestly and pretended to blush. Being an actress came in handy sometimes.

"An angel?" said her grandmother. "I'm not so sure about that."

"Whatever do you mean, Grandmama?" Molly asked innocently, putting a paw to her cheek.

"You were cavorting in the forest and on TV with that...that dogg."

"You mean Oscar? Oh, he's just a friend. He and I helped each other survive when we got lost in the wilderness and these weaselboars attacked us and—"

"He is a Montahugh!" shrieked Theodosia.

"Pardon me, Mother?" said Molly's father. "Did you say a...a...Montahugh?"

Molly's grandmother nodded sternly.

"Nyes. I did a little digging."

"In the litter box?" said Blade.

"No, Blade. I did research. In the hall of records." She pivoted, turning to Molly. "I found your 'friend' Oscar's dogg tag registration. His full name? Oscar Montahugh."

"But the Hissletons hate the Montahughs," said Molly's mother. "It's embroidered on all our pillows."

"I didn't know, Grandmama," said Molly.

Her grandmother arched a skeptical eyebrow. "About the pillows, dear?"

"No. About Oscar."

"Well, that's tinkle buried under the kitty litter now, dear. Kindly avoid any future contact with the horrible beast. We hate them. They hate us. Thus it has always been; thus it shall always be. Now, then, to the matter at hand. Boomer, your brother and his wife need your help. You and your family must put a stop to young Violet's impetuous romance. You must show her what life would be like if she were to follow her heart, marry an alley katt, and, thereby, toss away all the comforts she currently enjoys. I have come up with the purr-fect plan."

"I'm all ears, Mother dearest," said Molly's father. "Tell us what must be done."

"You, Boomer, and your family shall accompany Violet on a rugged backwoods adventure—with absolutely no pampering or mollycoddling allowed."

Another backwoods adventure? thought Molly. *No, thank you very much.*

Her grandmother kept going. "You four will rough it with Violet in this horrible Eastern Wilderness Reserve I've heard so many dreadful things about."

"Shouldn't my brother be the one 'roughing' it, as you say?" said Molly's father. "I chafe easily."

"I'm allergic to trees," said Blade. "They give me zits."

"Have I not made myself clear?" fumed Theodosia. "Your brother and his wife are at the end of their rope."

"Like in that katt poster?" said Blade. "The one that says 'Hang in There, Baby'?"

Theodosia ignored him. That happened a lot with Blade.

Molly was about to speak up. But her grandmother was glaring at her, her eyes daring Molly to say something against her plan. Molly swallowed hard. "I've already—"

"Oh, I know, Molly," said Theodosia, cutting her off. "You already did your wilderness adventure. With Oscar. *Oscar Montahugh*. But if you, or any of your family, wish to inherit any part of my fortune, you will do another wilderness adventure! This time with your cousin Violet!"

There was a slight pause as everyone did the math in their heads.

Without Theodosia's continued financial support, these Hissletons could, one day, wind up roaming around in an alley, scraping by on skeletal fish scraps, and joining Tom in his nightly howling at the moon.

"Of course we'll do it, Mother darling!" said Molly's father. "When should we leave?"

"Tomorrow. I will send my chauffeur to fetch Violet. And while you five tromp about in the brush and brambles, I will be arranging a more suitable romance for our dear, sweet Violet. I will organize an introduction to the richest, most eligible bachelor in all the land."

Molly gasped. She also urped a little. She'd seen photos of Kattsburgh's richest, most eligible bachelor in *Pawple* magazine. He definitely wasn't the best-looking bachelor in the land. Not by a long shot.

"Don't hate me because I'm handsome. Hate me because your girlfriend thinks I am."
Phineas Fatt

"You're, uh, not talking about Phineas Fatt, are you?" asked Molly, tasting a little hair ball at the back of her throat.

"Nyes," replied her grandmother haughtily. "I feel quite confident that Violet will forget all about her alley katt Tom after one miserable week in the woods. She'll long for the comforts only money can buy. She'll leap into Phineas Fatt's arms, bounce off his belly, and become his wife!"

Chapter 11

Oscar chased a slimy rubber ball his cousin Buster bounced across an open field.

It was his new favorite thing to do.

"Wow!" said Buster, watching Oscar tear through the meadow. "You're fast!"

"Oh, yes, I am!" said Oscar. He grabbed the ball, trotted back, and dropped the slippery thing in front of Buster. "I can run twenty-seven miles per hour. Most dogs can only do twenty-four. I'm the fastest player on my tennis ball team. Coach says I'm going to be first string this year!"

"Your drool is stringy, too!"

"Yes. Oh, yes, it is."

So far, Oscar had been having a blast at the Eastern Wilderness Reserve on the Montahugh Family Retreat. Yes, the place was kind of run-down. And shabby. And dilapidated—especially when compared to the Western Frontier Park. Instead of stainless steel water bowls, there were mud puddles. Instead of a dining hall where they made bacon and sausage melts, there was a tent filled with tins of dry dogg biscuits from the 1980s, and dehydrated beef stew. Still, he was having fun, romping around with his cousins—some of whom he only saw once or twice a year at dogg holidays, like January twenty-first, which was Squirrel Appreciation Day.

"You two!" shouted an angry voice. It was Grandpa Max. "Why are you tossing a ball?"

"Practice, sir," Buster shouted back. "In case a squirrel or a katt should venture into our dogg zone. We'll chase it down and grab it with our mouths and slobber all over it."

"Good answer, Buster. Oscar? Pay attention to your cousin. He's a real dogg!"

Grandpa Max moved on to yell at more members of his extended family.

"That was a lie," said Buster. "I like chasing after balls because it's fun."

"Yeah," said Oscar. "Me, too. Hey, Buster?"

"Yeah, Oscar?"

"How come Grandpa Max is so mad all the time?"

Buster shrugged. "Not sure. Maybe he has rabies. Or maybe..."

"What?"

"Well, this is just something I heard from Chompers. She's our second cousin twice removed."

"Why'd they remove her?" wondered Oscar. "And why'd they do it twice?"

Buster shrugged again. "I have absolutely no idea. Anyway, she says that years ago, back in the olden days, Grandpa Max had his heart broken."

"By a girl?"

Another shrug. "I guess. Could've been a clumsy cardiologist but I'm pretty sure Chompers was talking about, you know, mushy stuff."

"I hate mushy stuff."

"Yeah. Me, too. Except squishy balls."

"I love squishy balls," said Oscar, eagerly, which is how he usually said everything.

"I love squishy food, too!" said Buster.

"Let's go reconstitute some dehydrated beef stew!" suggested Oscar, eagerly, of course.

"Yum!" said Buster. "Muddy water gravy, here we come!"

Chapter 12

Oscar and Buster raced each other back to the base camp.

The food tent was in the center of the circle of pup tents that all the Montahugh doggs would be sharing during their rugged reunion week in the wilderness.

"I'm going to go grab my Dogg Scout camp cooking kit out of my tent," called Oscar.

"I'll go find some sticks for a fire!" shouted Buster, racing off into the woods.

"See you at the mess tent!" Oscar flipped up

the flap to his tent and sniffed something strong.

Cedar chips?

"Cousin Oscar!" gushed a dogg hidden in the shadows. "It's so grand to see you!"

Oscar's eyes adjusted to the darkness.

"Cousin Romaldo?"

"Yes! Fate has decreed that you and I are to be tentmates!"

"Seriously?"

"Well, not fate. It was that scruffy bear with the clipboard handing out tent assignments when you check in."

Oscar nodded. "His name is Bob. Bob the bear. He's in charge of all the campgrounds for all the different animal species."

Romaldo, who was dressed in a fancy ruffled costume instead of camping gear, clutched his paws to his heart. "You received my letter, I take it?"

"Yes. Clever code. That 'top secret' stamp."

"Yes. I thought so. You have to help me execute my clever plan, Cousin Oscar!"

Oscar nodded. "Sure. Let's start with the

clothes. I'd go with something a little more casual. Do you have any cargo shorts?"

"No. You must help me propose marriage to Violet!"

"I just learned that Violet is also coming here, to the Eastern Wilderness Reserve!" Romaldo said excitedly. "Her grandmother hopes to crush

Violet's spirit with a week of roughing it. For you see, Oscar, they think Violet is in love with an alley katt named Tom." He chuckled. "I made up that name."

Oscar nodded to be polite. "Oh. Clever."

"It worked. Oh, if her family knew with whom she is truly in love—me, a dogg—her family would be even more fur-rious. But true love shall triumph in the end. I have a plan!"

"Great. Well, good luck with that..."

"I need your assistance, Oscar. You're a clever Dogg Scout. I, frankly, am a klutz when it comes to traipsing through the trees or fording streams. You, on the other hand, know how to make your way through the wilderness with ease, as you did with your girlfriend Molly, the katt."

"She's not my—"

"Oscar, I need you to hike through the forest, enter katt territory, and deliver my secret message to fair, sweet Violet. She will be so near, and yet so far!"

"Um, can I get back to you on this? Buster and I have a date with a bowl of dehydrated beef stew."

"But—"

"Catch you later, Romaldo."

Romaldo gave Oscar his saddest puppy dogg eyes.

Which Oscar ignored as he bolted out of the tent to go spend time with a cousin who wasn't so sappy and goofy.

Chapter 13

Cousin Violet arrived at the Hissleton home early in the morning.

"Is there, like, coffee or espresso or something?" she asked. "I'm not a morning katt."

"Who is, dear?" said Molly's mom, stretching into yet another yawn. "Who is?"

Molly's dad had reminded Molly and Blade that their cousin wasn't "the sharpest claw in the paw."

"I'm not saying the girl is an airhead," he told them. "But that twinkle in her eye? I believe it might come from someone shining a flashlight into her ear."

Blade cracked up. Molly rolled her eyes. Her father could be such an oaf sometimes.

Grandmother Hissleton had left the night before. She was off to have "a few words" about the future with Phineas Fatt's family. "I'm sure they'll recognize the financial benefits of the romantic merger I'm proposing," she'd said. "The Hissletons and the Fatts. Together we could rule all of Kattsburgh."

Molly's grandmother was always scheming. Scheming was what family matriarchs did best, she said.

Violet had apologized when the limo dropped her off (with about a dozen suitcases and trunks) two hours later than scheduled.

"Sorry. I was in the shower forever because the shampoo bottle said *lather, rinse, repeat*, so I did. Several times."

While Molly's father and Blade loaded up the SUV for the drive to the Eastern Wilderness

Reserve, Molly and Violet had what Violet called a "private girl talk" in Molly's room.

"Is that what you're wearing to the wilderness?" Violet asked when they were alone.

"I guess," said Molly, who was dressed in her best "let's go camping" khaki safari clothes.

"Interesting," said Violet. "I was thinking about a more exotic look. The wilderness makes me think of lions and tigers and leopards. I might go with stripes or spots. Maybe a fluffy full-mane wig."

"Um, how many outfits did you pack?"

"Dozens. One can never have too many clothes or jewels, am I right, girlfriend?"

I love wearing sparkly things. Then I can chase my own reflections on the walls!

"Sooooo," said Violet, making a rapid-fire series of cutesy-kitty facial expressions and jiggling her sequined collar. "Tell me all about your boyfriend, Oscar."

"He's not my boyfriend."

Violet winked. "Sure. I understand. It's hard for a katt to be in love with a dogg. There's so much negativity. Haters gonna hate, am I right?"

"Oscar and I aren't in love."

"Oh, no. Did you two break up?"

"No. We never were a couple. We were just friends."

"Sure." Violet gave her another wink. "Your secret is safe with me, girlfriend. I saw how you kissed him on TV."

"That was just for show. See, I'm going to be an actress so I need to be able to pretend stuff."

"Riiiiight. Got it. Oh, by the way, if we order pizza for lunch, let's have them slice it into six pieces instead of twelve. I could never eat twelve."

Molly nodded. "Mom? Dad?" she hollered. "Is it time to go?"

"Yes, dear!" said her father. "The car is loaded.

All of Violet's luggage is now safely on board. Be sure you two use the litter box before we depart. We're not stopping at any rest stops along the way!"

"Molly?" whispered Violet.

"Um, yeah?" Molly whispered back.

"I'm so glad you're on my team."

"Okay. What team is that?"

"Team Love, sister. Team Love!"

Violet gave Molly a pair of *mwah!* air-kisses and skipped out of the room.

Molly might've followed her. But after all that lovey-dovey talk, she was too busy hocking up a hair ball.

Chapter 14

Molly's father piloted the family's SUV up the bumpy, potholed road into the Eastern Wilderness Reserve.

The park's welcome sign was missing a few letters. It read EAT WILD ERVE. Weeds and vines choked the flower beds where all the petals were brown and wilted.

"My goodness," said Molly's father. "This place is a dump."

"What's an erve?" asked Blade. "I like to know what I'm eating, especially if it's wild."

"Can we go home now?" asked Violet. "I think I'm allergic to natural stuff like nature."

"You're the reason we're here, dear," Molly's mother reminded Violet.

"Nyes," said her father. "I feel quite certain there won't be any alley katts named Tom here amid the trees because, as you can clearly see, there aren't any alleys."

"But I love...*Tom*," said Violet with, Molly noticed, the hint of a stifled giggle. Plus, it almost sounded like she was saying the name "Tom" in air quotes.

"Well, the sooner you get over this Tom Katt, my dear niece," said Molly's father, "the sooner we can all go home!"

The car jounced along the rutted dirt road until they came to a gatehouse. The guardrail, made out of a bumpy log, was blocking the way forward. Molly's father rolled down his window.

"Excuse me?" he called out. "Guests checking in. Boomer Hissleton the Third, Esquire."

There was no reply.

"Hello? Can someone kindly raise this gate?" He tooted his horn. Nothing happened. "This is ridiculous. I demand to speak to a manager!"

Finally, an old brown bear leisurely strolled out of the ramshackle gatehouse. He wore a green uniform shirt that strained against its buttons, and had a big belly that sagged over the beltline of his green work pants. He was also munching on an oozing honeycomb with one paw. Sticky stuff was splattered all over his furry face and dribbling down to stain his work shirt.

"Hang on, chief," the bear said to Molly's father. "Don't get your whiskers twisted in a knot." He chomped another crunchy bite out of the honeycomb. "What can I do you for?"

"We're the Hissletons."

"Oh," said the bear with a not at all subtle wink. "No wonder you were throwing a hissy fit. In fact, I'd say you were getting hiss-sterical. Heh-heh-heh. I find a little levity can often lighten an otherwise tense situation. How about you?"

Molly's father wasn't in the mood for levity. "We have reservations."

"So do I. But, I'll probably let you camp here, anyhow. Heh-heh-heh."

"We're scheduled to camp here all week," said Molly's father, who was not at all amused by the big brown bear. "Heaven help us."

"Okay," said the bear, who seemed to be switching to autopilot to give his standard check-in spiel. "I'm Bob. I am the superintendent here at the Eastern Wilderness Reserve. That means I am the captain of this particular landlocked ship. As you should know, if you read our brochure or visited our website—where user comments and/or reviews are always discouraged—the wilderness is blocked off into strict, single-species zones. For instance, I sleep in the bear zone. Why? Because I'm a bear. You folks appear to be katts, am I correct?"

"Nyes."

"What gave us away?" snarked Blade from the back seat. "Our ears or our tails?"

"Neither," said the bear, totally unfazed. "It was mostly your smell. Do all katt butts smell like cheese? Anyhoo. We have a strict segregation policy. Katts camp with katts. Doggs camp with doggs. Muskrats camp with muskrats. Marsupials—"

"We get the idea!" snapped Molly's father.

"Ooh. Easy, big fella," chuckled the bear. "You don't want to have a heart attack and waste one of your nine lives. You might need them for a video game. Now, like I said, there are zones and sectors and boundary lines. Do not cross over into another species' territory, zone, or sector. If you do, you will be asked to leave the Eastern Wilderness Reserve. If, of course, you are still alive. Some of our guests? Whooo. They're total animals. They've got claws and teeth and aren't afraid to use them."

"What about the doggs?" asked Violet. "Where are they?"

"Don't worry, little missy. We know you katts hate doggs and the doggs hate you. That's why there's a wide river separating the katt zone from the dogg zone. Just don't cross it, and you'll be fine."

With a grunt and a groan, he finally opened the gate. "Enjoy your stay. Or, at least, try not to get a rash."

"Thank you, good sir!" said Molly's father. "Let our wilderness adventure begin!"

Oh, joy, thought Molly. *Camping with fussy Cousin Violet.*

She couldn't wait for this week to be over.

Chapter 15

Oscar and his family joined the rest of the Montahugh doggs around a blazing campfire.

Grandpa Max was about to make a speech.

Then they could roast hot dogs on sticks. Oscar loved hot dogs. Hated the name. Reminded him that he had to wear a fur coat. In August.

"Tomorrow," said Grandpa Max, "we'll continue to remember what it means to be a dogg. We'll chase things. We'll sniff things. We'll bark our fool heads off if we have something to bark about. Maybe we'll even learn a few new tricks. And if some katt should make the mistake of venturing across the river…"

Oscar wagged his tail. He knew this one. He had a katt merit badge.

"They won't, Grandpa Max," he said. "Katts hate water. Oh, yes they do. I studied kattology for my Dogg Scout katt merit badge."

Grandpa Max glared at him. The flickering light from the campfire flames made him look even angrier. Spookier, too.

But Oscar kept going. "Since katts constantly groom themselves with their tongues and remove so much oil from their fur, their coats are fluffier and less waterproof than ours. So they feel cold and their fur feels heavier if they get wet. So don't worry. No katts will be swimming our way."

Oscar was wagging his tail in quick, short strokes. He was anxious. He hoped Grandpa Max liked his answer.

Grandpa Max did not.

"I assume all of you know about my grandson Oscar."

The doggs circling the firepit grumbled.

"He's the one who disgraced our family by saving a Hissleton. Quick refresher course: As doggs, we hate katts. But as Montahughs? We hate Hissletons even more!"

The circle of doggs howled and barked and yipped in agreement. Even Oscar's mom, dad, and big sister were hooting along with the mob. The only one not joining the chorus was Cousin Romaldo. He shot Oscar a wink and mouthed four words: *We. Need. To. Talk!*

That night, in their shared pup tent, they did.

"She's here!" whispered Romaldo.

"Who's here?" asked Oscar.

"Violet!" He wiggle-waggled his phone in his paw. "She just texted me. She and her family set up camp over in the katt section today! Woofhoo!"

Romaldo was so excited, he tossed his phone up in the air and did a happy dance.

"You have to go find her, Oscar!" said Romaldo when his happy dancing was done.

"Huh?"

"It's phase one of my brilliant master plan. Use your Dogg Scout skills and bring Violet my top secret message of love."

"Couldn't you just text her back?"

Romaldo gasped as if he were horrified by Oscar's suggestion. "Make a marriage proposal via text? Tsk-tsk-tsk. That is just not done, Oscar. It's bad form."

"Oh. I did not know that. But Violet's over in the katt section. Across the river. No doggs allowed."

"Yes—the course of love never did run smooth…"

Oscar nodded. "Especially if there are raging rapids in the river. Then it's kind of choppy."

"I have written Violet this love poem!" said Romaldo, unfurling a piece of parchment and reading the poetry stretching down the scroll. It was one of those free verse things Oscar had studied in school. It was a mess and made very little sense.

My dearest Violet
Eyes of gray
Ears of white
Truly
My own
Eyes have never beheld…

Oscar raised a paw to cut off Romaldo before he read enough to make Oscar hurl. "Oh-kay. I think I've got the gist of it…"

"Play Cupid for me, Oscar. Use all that you learned from your time in the wilderness with Molly and hand-deliver my poem. I'd do it myself, but…"

"Good idea," said Oscar before Romaldo could give him his "but."

"Please, Oscar?" pleaded Romaldo. "Cross the river and head over to the Hissleton katt encampment."

Now Oscar was confused.

"Why should I look for the Hissletons?" he asked.

"Because Violet is a Hissleton. Her name is Violet Hissleton."

Grandpa Max was mad enough at Oscar already. He didn't want to make things worse by messing with the Hissletons. *Again.*

He slapped his paw to his forehead.

"Doy! I nearly forgot. My dad and I are supposed to sleep under the stars together tonight. It's a father-son bonding thing. He's going to show me how to find the dogg star. The tent is all yours, Romaldo."

"B-b-but…"

"En-joy!"

Oscar grabbed his toothbrush and scampered off to find a pile of pine needles to sleep in for the night. Anything to get away from his love-crazed cousin Romaldo.

It took a while, but eventually he fell asleep beneath a blanket of twinkling stars.

Hours later, as the morning sun was warming his snout, Oscar awoke to a chorus of barks.

His cousin Buster came running up to him, panting hard.

"Hey, Oscar, guess what?"

"What?"

"We're going on a hunt!"

"We are?"

"Yep. The whole family. Cousin Romaldo is missing."

Chapter 16

This is a great opportunity for us all," Grandpa Max growled when the whole clan gathered in the mess hall (which really was a mess because, well, doggs). "A chance to practice our sniffing, hunting, and tracking skills. Because we are doggs, ladies and gentlemen. Finding missing things is what we do!"

Oscar was with his family near the front of the room. He had a sheepish look on his face and a guilty, gurgly feeling in his stomach. He had an idea of where Cousin Romaldo may have gone.

Across the river to the katt zone so he could deliver a sappy poem to Violet Hissleton.

"Here is a map of the whole dadburn Eastern Wilderness Reserve," said Grandpa, unfurling and spreading out a map the size of a beach towel on one of the tables. Oscar went up on tippy-claws to check it out. He couldn't believe how many different red-lined zones there were. One for doggs and one for katts, of course. Those were separated by a wide river. But there were also regions for squirrels, skunks, monkeys, sheep, foxes, shrews, buffalo, and something called a binturong. Oscar counted a hundred different segregated sectors for a hundred different species before he lost count. (He was never very good at math.)

"Romaldo has to be somewhere in the dogg district," said Grandpa Max, tapping his paw on the map.

"He darn well better be!" said Oscar's father, Duke. "It's against every Wilderness Reserve rule for any species to stray outside its zone."

"Romaldo isn't a stray," said Romaldo's mother defensively.

"That's not what I meant, Beulah. Ah, never mind. I'm just saying Romaldo better stick to his own zone."

"Who has a stick?" said about six puppies.

Grandpa Max cleared his throat. Loudly.

"Enough! We need to find Romaldo. And, yes, he will be somewhere here in the dogg sector. Nothing personal, Beulah, but your son is too chicken to venture into any other creatures' zones."

"What about the one for poultry?" said Fifi, trying to be helpful.

Grandpa Max rolled his eyes.

"What?" said Fifi. "You said he was chicken."

Grandpa Max shifted his glare to Oscar's mother. "Lola? Muzzle your daughter. Time's

87

wasting. Romaldo is probably here." He tapped the northernmost tip of the dogg zone. "The dogg-wood forest."

"My poor puppy!" whined his mother. "Romaldo won't last long. He's more of a city dogg. Romaldo's used to his food coming out of cans, not nature."

He's also a terrible Dogg Scout, thought Oscar. *And the woods can be a dark and dangerous place.* Oscar knew that for a fact. He and Molly barely survived their adventure.

"Whoever finds Romaldo wins a five-pound sack of bully sticks!" announced Grandpa. "So start sniffing!"

"Here's a pair of his underpants," said Romaldo's mother, holding up a set of boxer shorts decorated with valentine hearts. "Get a good whiff!"

All the doggs took turns stepping up, wiggling their nostrils, and recording Romaldo's scent. Oscar recognized the smell. Cedar. Wood chips. With a hint of vanilla.

When everybody was finished smelling the undershorts, Grandpa Max proclaimed, "The race to find Romaldo begins...NOW!"

The whole Montahugh family took off, racing north, heading toward the doggwood forest.

Oscar was the only one who slipped off to the west.

He had to rescue Romaldo. From the katt zone.

Because it was his fault that Romaldo had gone over there in the first place.

Chapter 17

Oscar could hear the river before he could see it.

It sounded like a roaring lion that could roar forever without taking a break or running out of breath.

Speaking of lions, he thought. *Where are they? With the other katts? In their own lion zone?*

Oscar did not want to meet any new lions, thank you very much. A mountain lion had stalked Oscar and Molly in the Western Frontier Park. It had even taken a bite out of Molly's tail and torn Oscar's backpack to shreds.

Going into the katt section was dangerous enough. Stepping foot inside lion territory? That would just be stupid.

Oscar worked his way through some burr bushes and thorny brambles. His father, mother, and sister had stuck with the pack and dashed north. That was a good thing. He didn't need them telling him how foolishly he was behaving. He could do that for himself.

Oscar slid down a slick bank to the river's mucky edge. His fur was a mess. His butt was muddy. The river in front of him was wide and swift.

"Oscar?" hollered a familiar voice. "Is that you?"

It was Molly! She was on the other side.

"Hiya, Molly!" he shouted back. "Wowzers, I am so glad to see you again!"

Molly crossed her arms over her chest and shot him a look. "Oh, really? Why? So your sister can hurl more insults at me?"

Oscar's tail drooped and he dropped his head in shame as he remembered the last time he'd seen Molly. That awful ride home from the Western Frontier Park.

He cupped his paws over his snout and said as loudly as he could, "I'm sorry about all those dumb things Fifi shouted about you. None of them were true."

"I know that, Oscar! I'm me, remember?"

"Yeah. You know more about you than Fifi does."

Molly uncrossed her arms. "So why *are* you here?"

"I'm looking for my cousin Romaldo. He's missing. I think he might've snuck over there to, uh, meet his girlfriend. Her name is Violet."

"Violet Hissleton?"

"Yeah! That's right. How'd you know?"

"She's my cousin, Oscar. And she's in love with an alley katt named Tom."

"Nope. She's in love with my cousin. Romaldo."

Molly stomped her feet. "I knew it! Of course she was making that junk up. An alley katt named Tom: Tom Katt. How stupid does she think I am?"

She stopped for a second. "Wait a minute. My cousin is in love with *your* cousin?"

"Yes!" said Oscar. "And he's a dogg."

"Great!" said Molly, throwing up both arms. "Well, guess what? My cousin Violet is missing, too."

"No. Way!"

"Yes. Way. I was kind of searching for her."

"Well, I'm definitely searching for my cousin Romaldo. In fact, my whole family is trying to track him down. It's like our group activity for the day. Tomorrow, we might do crafts or put on a talent show..."

"Do you think your cousin crossed the river to meet my cousin?" asked Molly.

"Yeah," panted Oscar. "I do. I really do. Because, last night, instead of just texting Violet, Romaldo wanted me to come over there and hand-deliver a lovey-dovey poem to her but I said no because mushy stuff grosses me out. Plus, it's against the rules for doggs to go into katt territory. I'm only thinking about doing it now because, well,

Romaldo is the worst Dogg Scout ever. He could get lost or hurt or worse."

"Violet's not very woodsy, either," said Molly. "This morning, she asked me where she could find a beaver to nibble on her nails and give her a pawdecure. She and Romaldo might've made a secret pact to meet each other over here, on this side of the river."

"Really?" puzzled Oscar. "Why not over here?"

"Because, Oscar, everything's nicer in the katt zone. For one thing, there are no doggs yelling mean things. For another, over here we bury our poop."

True, thought Oscar. Things could get extremely odiferous in the dogg zone. You had to watch where you stepped, too. Sometimes you got a squishy surprise.

"Okay," he said. "I'm coming over. We'll organize a search party."

"We will?" said Molly.

"Yeah. But you and me will be the only ones invited to the party!"

Chapter 18

Molly heard urgent footfalls behind her.

"Oscar!" she shouted. "Wait! Someone's coming!"

Oscar gave her a big paws-up. He understood. He ducked into a bush.

"Ouch!" Molly heard him yelp.

It must've been a sticker bush.

"There you are, Molly dearest!" Her father came huffing and puffing through the trees, which were slapping him in the face with their leaves. "Nasty trees. Why must they have these branchy things and so many pesky leaves?"

"Is everything okay, Dad?"

"Yes, dumpling. Now that I know you haven't been katt-napped along with your cousin Violet."

"Katt-napped?"

"Nyes. The park ranger just discovered a set of dogg paw prints traipsing into our campground!"

Bob, the bear with the bloated belly, came through the trees, hiking up his green work pants.

"Superintendent," said Bob.

"Excuse me?" purred Molly's father.

"I'm not a park ranger, Whiskers. I'm the superintendent. Means I'm the big kahuna. The head honcho. Mister Cheese." The bear turned to Molly. He had crusted honey gook under his snout. "Anyway, little lady…"

Oooh. That made Molly mad. She hated when anybody called her a little lady.

"…I did find a fresh set of dogg paw prints near your campsite. Leads me to suspect that a dogg snatched your cousin. Probably holding her for ransom. Might ask you people for a year's supply of peanut butter biscuits for her safe return. Maybe some rawhide chews."

Molly, of course, now knew that a dogg hadn't katt-napped Violet. If what Oscar said was true, Violet had run off to be with her boyfriend, Romaldo the dogg.

"Excuse me, sir?" she said to the bear.

"Yes, little missy?"

Inside, Molly seethed. Outside, she smiled. She was an actress. She could pretend that the bumbling bear hadn't just offended her even though he totally had.

"Were there katt paw prints alongside those of the dogg? Any signs of a struggle?"

"Nope. I figure the katt-napper hoisted your cousin off the ground and carried her away."

Or, thought Molly, *the dogg came looking for Violet but she was already gone. She might've even ventured across the river to meet her boyfriend on the dogg side. Maybe she wrote him a sappy poem, too!*

"Heavens, sir," Molly's father said to the bear, "aren't the doggs legally obligated to stay on their side of the river?"

"Yeah. Those are the rules and regulations," said the bear with a shrug. "But sometimes you get your mavericks. Especially over in the cattle zone. Mavericks are always jumping the fence to herd the cows..."

"Exactly how many sectors are there?" asked Molly.

"Too many if you ask me, which you did, which is why I answered. Anyhoo, I'll mosey over to the dogg section after lunch, have a word with them. See if anyone is missing."

"Why can't you do that now?" asked Molly's father.

"I'm a busy bear, pal. Got all sorts of interspecies disputes to look into." He pulled a spiral notebook out of his work shirt pocket. "For instance, we have a goat butting heads with a buffalo, not to mention a squirrel going nuts in the chipmunk zone."

"Aren't they both rodents?" said Molly. "Can't they just get along?"

"You'd think so, wouldn't you? Enjoy the rest of your day, folks. And be on the lookout for renegade doggs."

That made Molly glance across the river to the far shore. Her own renegade dogg, Oscar, was still safely hidden in his prickly bush.

The bear lumbered away. Molly's father scurried along after him.

"We should photograph those paw prints! Make a plaster cast mold. It will help us identify the perpetrator."

"You watch those CSI shows on TV, am I right?"

Molly heard the bear ask as he and her father walked away.

"Indeed, I do..."

Molly waited until she was sure they were gone.

Then she cupped her hands over her snout again and called out, "Oscar? Oscar?"

Oscar worked his way out of the shrub that seemed glued to his fur like thorny Velcro.

"Everything okay, Molly?" he asked eagerly.

"Yes. Now. But maybe you shouldn't—"

"Okay. I'm coming over."

"No, Oscar. Wait..."

But Molly was too late. Oscar hopped into the stream and started dogg-paddling his way toward the center of the river.

Where the current looked swift.

Very, very swift.

Chapter 19

*W*e have to find Romaldo! thought Oscar as he churned through the water, all four legs pumping. *Molly and I can do it. We're a good team. Oh, yes, we are!*

Oscar was thinking about how they could follow Romaldo's scent and maybe find his paw prints and track him down and bring him back to the dogg zone, maybe before lunch. But when he got to the middle of the river, Oscar realized he probably should've been thinking more about swimming than hunting.

Because, all of a sudden, the river had picked up speed. The swift current was tugging him sideways—sliding Oscar away from Molly and the distant shore, which was becoming even more distant as he drifted downstream. No matter how hard he thrashed his legs or churned his arms, the water wouldn't let Oscar go where he wanted.

He was trapped in the current!

"Help!" he yelped. "Little help!"

Now he was bobbing up and down like one of those red-and-white bobbers on a fishing line. River water was gurgling in his mouth. When he came up for air, he twisted around and looked over his shoulder.

Molly was gone! Did she go with her father and the bear?

Did she abandon him?

Maybe. Probably. She sounded as if she was still pretty sore about all that mean stuff Fifi had hollered at her.

The water turned choppy and was capped with

white foam. Oscar was in a surge of rapids, which would explain why he was being whisked downstream so rapidly! He needed to turn around. To see where he was going. To make sure there wasn't a waterfall up ahead.

There was!

Oscar could hear it roar. Now the river sounded like a thousand angry lions as its white water sluiced under a fallen tree and cascaded over a cliff in a curve of sudsy bubbles.

Oscar struggled and kicked and flailed. But he couldn't fight the current.

This is it, he thought, closing his eyes, letting the river take him wherever it wanted to go. *I wish I were a katt. Then I'd have eight more lives after I lose this one.*

"Open your eyes, you idiot!" screamed Molly.

Oscar popped open an eyelid.

Molly was on the fallen tree straddling the raging rapids. She had her arms dangling off the edge, her claws exposed to make a furry grappling hook.

104

Oscar had to fight against the current to raise one arm.

He passed under the fallen tree limb.

Molly grabbed hold of his shirtsleeve with the sharp, hooked tips of all five extended claws. The shirt fabric didn't rip. Molly yanked hard.

Oscar popped up out of the rapids, dug his claws into the tree bark, and hauled himself to safety.

It took a moment for Oscar to catch his breath. And to spit out all the river water he'd just swallowed.

Finally, when he could speak, he did. "Thank you, Molly. You really are my best friend in the whole wide world. None of my other friends have ever saved my life. Thank you, thank you, thank you!"

"You're welcome, Oscar," said Molly with a soft chuckle. "And Oscar?"

"Yeah, Molly?"

"Do me a favor."

"Sure. Anything!"

"Don't shake yourself dry until I'm at least fifteen feet away."

"You got it!"

Molly scampered nimbly along the sideways tree to the riverbank. When she was safely in the forest, Oscar stood up, gave his coat a good shimmy, and sent droplets of dirty river water slinging in all directions. Coat dry, he scampered, a little less nimbly than Molly had, to the safety of the shore.

"That was certainly exciting," Oscar told Molly, wagging his tail excitedly. "Like being inside a runaway washing machine in the rinse and spin cycles. So is this the katt zone?"

Molly looked around. She didn't recognize any landmarks.

"I don't think so. The river carried you pretty far downstream. I was running so fast, I wasn't paying attention to where I was or any of the posted signs and warnings about border crossings."

Suddenly, the reunited friends heard a blow and a snort and galloping hooves.

"Is that a horse?" asked Molly.

"No. It sounds bigger than a horse," said Oscar, peering into the forest. "Much, much bigger."

And then he saw it. Three thousand pounds of thick-skinned muscle charging through the wilderness with its head down and its curved tusk aimed at Oscar and Molly.

"Yikes!" yelped Oscar. "I think we ended up in the rhinoceros zone!"

Chapter 20

Oscar was dismayed by how many angry creatures there were, not only in the world, but also in the Eastern Wilderness Reserve.

Everybody wanted their own territory and became furious if someone different dared to stumble across their border.

"Run faster!" he coached Molly.

"I can't!" she shouted back. "Remember?"

"Oh. Right. I forgot. Hop on my back. I'm the fastest dogg on my tennis ball team."

"Too bad the thing charging after us isn't a tennis ball!"

Molly sprang up off the ground in mid-stride and landed on Oscar's back.

"Yikes!" Oscar winced. "Um, could you retract your claws a little bit? They're kind of puncturing my skin."

"These are the same claws that just saved your life, Oscar. Back at the waterfall?"

"You're right. I owe them. Dig in."

"Oscar?"

"Yeah?"

"I can feel hot rhino breath on the back of my neck. Can we run a little faster?"

Oscar chanced a look over his shoulder. The rhino was pounding along, stomping the ground with its sledgehammer hooves, puffing up thick clouds of dust. Molly was right. The beast was gaining on them. *Of course*, Oscar thought, *the rhino probably doesn't think of itself as a beast. It probably thinks we're the beasts because we're the ones who rudely invaded its territory. We came to its party without an invitation. We took a shortcut through its backyard without asking.*

"Oscar?" shrieked Molly.

"Yeah?" panted Oscar.

"Are you thinking about stuff again?"

"Sort of!"

"Well, knock it off and run. Faster!"

"You got it."

Oscar kicked it up a gear. Coach would've been proud. Oscar was clipping along at twenty-seven miles per hour. Unfortunately, he knew that a black rhinoceros could do *thirty-four*. Sometimes, Oscar hated when he knew stuff.

He could feel warm puffs of damp rhino breath blasting against his butt. He knew without looking that he and Molly were about to be gored. Skewered on the rhino's curved horn like katt and dogg shish kebab.

"There!" shouted Molly. "The border."

Oscar squinted and read the bright-yellow signs posted on a line of trees spreading out in both directions. KATTS ONLY. NO RHINOS ALLOWED BEYOND THIS POINT.

Maybe I can do thirty-four, too! thought Oscar as he sprinted for the finish line. The instant they cleared the border, they heard the charging rhino skid to a stop by digging in its stumpy feet and bulldozing through the dirt. It finally slid to rest with the tip of its horn maybe six inches from a tree with one of the yellow *no trespassing*–type signs nailed to it.

"Stay out and don't never come back!" the rhinoceros roared. "We're on vacation over here!"

"Sorry, sir," said Oscar. "My mistake. Won't happen again."

"Ha!" snorted the rhino. "It already has."

"Excuse me?" said Molly. "We're not in your territory. This is the katt zone."

"I know," huffed the rhino. "But, just in case you hadn't noticed, that creature you're riding is a dogg! First he invades our space, next he slips into yours. That dogg is an interloper and an intruder."

"Nah," said Molly, hopping off Oscar's back. "He's just an Oscar. And he's my friend."

That made Oscar's ears go warm and fuzzy. "Aw, thanks, Molly."

"Ha!" laughed the rhino. "With friends like that,

who needs enemies? Oh, but he is your enemy. Your sworn enemy for life!" The rhino blasted some kind of bugle call through his enormous nose. "Hey, katts in the next zone?" he shouted. "Yoo-hoo! Wake up from your kattnaps! You're being invaded by a mangy dogg!"

Chapter 21

Oh, great," said Molly as the rhino kept horn-butting trees on his side of the border, making their canopy of leaves rustle loudly. "It's nap time, but he's turning the whole forest into a giant leafy green alarm clock. Come on!"

"Um, where are we going?" asked Oscar.

"Away from here. That big, bullheaded battering ram is going to wake up every katt in the zone. It's against the rules for you to be here, Oscar."

"Yeah, but you wouldn't come over to the dogg

zone and we need to find Romaldo and Violet."

"Shhh!" whispered Molly. "I have a new clue. I'll fill you in on the way."

"The way to where?" Oscar whispered back.

"The supposed scene of the crime. My family's campsite."

Molly stealthily slipped around trees and bushes on katt paws. Oscar tried to do the same. It was more difficult on dogg paws.

"Shouldn't we be looking for a place to hide?" wondered Oscar as he followed Molly.

"There's no time to hide. We just have to be very, very careful."

"Good point. Besides, you really can't find someone if you're, you know, hiding."

"Okay. Here's what I've learned. Superintendent Bob, that big boor of a bear, found some dogg paw prints behind our camper. He assumes that Romaldo katt-napped Violet. I asked him if there were any katt paw prints alongside those of the dogg and he said no. His theory is that the katt-napper carried Cousin Violet away, struggling in his arms."

"He's wrong," said Oscar. "My cousin Romaldo is sort of weak. Very little upper body strength. I had to help him carry his kibble tray in the dining hall because it was too heavy for him."

"Well," said Molly, "I think Romaldo snuck into our campsite, probably late last night, hoping to rendezvous with Violet."

"Because I refused to deliver his love poem. So he decided to sneak over here and do it himself!"

"But when he got here," said Molly, sounding like a detective, "Violet was already gone."

Oscar gasped in anticipation. "Where'd she go?"

Molly shook her head. "That's the part I don't know. Not yet, anyway. But I think she found a way to tell him where to meet her."

"A text! They text a lot. Well, Violet likes to text. Romaldo likes to pen love poems. The kind without any rhymes, or pattern, or form. It's just poetry because people say it's poetry. I think they call it free verse. Even though Romaldo's love poems are so bad, I don't think you could even give them away for free. Why, they're so bad—"

Molly held up her right paw to signal Oscar to freeze and keep quiet. She put a curved claw to her lips. "Shhh. Someone's coming."

Chapter 22

Y ou've got good ears!" Oscar whispered to Molly.

"You like them? I always thought they were too pointy. Like tiny tortilla chips."

"I mean you can hear good."

"Oh. Yeah. Duh. Quick, hide behind that rock."

Oscar ducked behind a moss-speckled boulder.

"Ah, there you are, Molly dearest," boomed her father, working his way up a narrow path. He was followed by Blaze.

"We just received an intruder alert," said Blaze,

licking his paws eagerly. "From the rhinos next door."

"The way they were shaking their trees," said her father, "we suspect a dogg has been spotted in the katt zone!"

"A dogg?" Molly gasped melodramatically. "Oh, no!"

"Oh, yes, dear. We fear the dastardly dogg katt-napper is on the prowl for his next victim. Your mother has locked herself in her room and is hiding inside a cardboard box. You should do the same."

"Well, what are you two going to do?" Molly asked.

"We're going hunting!" said Blaze. "And if we see a dogg, it'll be scratch first, ask questions later."

"Oh, I'm so afraid, Father," said Molly, pretending to swoon a little. "I'm young. I'm pretty. The katt-napper might come for me. I think I would feel safer hiding somewhere where nobody would ever think to look for me."

"And where is that, sugarplum?"

"I can't tell you."

"Riiiight," said Blaze. "If you did, we would know where to think to look for you!"

"Exactly, Blaze. You're a genius!"

Blaze beamed. "I know. It's so totally true."

"Very well, Molly, dearest," said her father. "Do as you must. Hide somewhere safe but do rejoin us for dinner. We're having the three S's—snapper, salmon, and sardines."

"Can't wait!"

"Come along, son. We need to find a dirty, sneaky, cousin-snatching dogg."

Molly's father and brother hiked off into the woods, two katts on a mission.

"Okay," Molly said when they were gone. "This is great. I don't have to be home until suppertime. We can use that time to find Violet and Romaldo. Come on, Oscar."

Oscar peeked out from behind the boulder. "Where are we going?"

"To my camper. I need to pull together a disguise. A costume," Molly mumbled as she thought out loud. "I'll have to borrow that wig Dad packed for the closing campfire talent show. The one that makes him look like a lion. He was going to sing that 'a-weema-weh' song. Again. Anyway, lions are allowed to visit the katt zone...they're cousins..."

"Um, Molly? Why do you need a costume?"

She laughed. "It's not for me, Oscar. It's for you."

"What?"

"Every katt in this zone is out there hunting for a dogg. Fine. We need to turn you into a katt! A BIG katt. Nobody will mess with a visiting king of the jungle!"

Chapter 23

"Do I really have to wear this?" asked Oscar.

He was checking out his reflection in the chrome hubcap of the Hissleton family's recreational vehicle. He had on a fluffy lion's mane headpiece, complete with pointy ears. He was also wearing a HELLO KATTY T-shirt over his own shirt plus a pair of Molly's brother's jeans, which were so snug in the rear end they seriously limited his tail-wagging abilities.

"Yes, Oscar. You need to pretend to be a young lion visiting your distant katt relatives."

"But I look ridiculous."

"You'd look worse with claw scars all over your face."

Oscar thought about that. "You make a very good point. Okay, where did Superintendent Bob find the dogg paw prints?"

"Back here," said Molly, leading the way.

Oscar saw several very clear paw impressions in the dry, caked clay behind the parked camper. He bent down and gave the tracks a good sniff. "Oh, yeah. That's Romaldo. I smelled his underpants. He smells like a cedar chest where someone dropped a scoop of vanilla ice cream. I think he uses a body spray. And look," said Oscar, pointing to where a sunbeam was spotlighting more paw prints. "He went that way!"

Molly gasped. "We didn't see those before."

"Probably because that sunbeam wasn't spotlighting them."

"You're right. Looks like your cousin Romaldo was headed west."

"What's to the west?"

"The giraffe zone," said Molly, leading the way.

"Their heads poke out above the treetops. They're extremely tall."

"Yeah," said Oscar. "They're giraffes."

Oscar and Molly hiked for almost a mile. The katt sector, like the doggs', was wide. Oscar's tongue was hanging out of his mouth, flapping and dribbling. As they neared the border between the zones, he started seeing the familiar yellow signs posted on a staggered line of trees: GIRAFFE ZONE. NO KATTS ALLOWED BEYOND THIS POINT.

"Hey, looky there, George," said a reedy voice over Oscar's head. "It's the king of the jungle, traipsing around in the woods!"

"Ha!" laughed a second high-pitched voice. "Must be here visiting cousins."

Oscar shielded his eyes from the sun and stared straight up. There were two giraffes, their mouths working like washing machines as they chewed leaves they'd just nibbled off the tops of nearby trees.

"Maybe he can help them catch the dogg!" said the one.

"Good point, Gertrude," said the other, chomping into another clump of green. "Good point, indeed."

"What did you say about a dogg?" Molly shouted up to her katt zone neighbors.

"Hey, we're not nosy," said Gertrude.

"Nope," said George. "But we're very necky. We keep our heads up. We see stuff."

"And late last night or maybe early this morning," said Gertrude. "We saw a dogg in a puffy-sleeved shirt slinking through your woods."

Oscar gasped. "That's Romaldo," he whispered to Molly. "All he wears are puffy-sleeved shirts. And tights. Sometimes he wears tights. He looks like a pirate."

"We're looking for that dogg," Molly said to the giraffes.

"That why you brought in a lion?" asked George.

"Uh, yeah. Lions are good hunters."

"Ha! Tell me about it," said Gertrude. "I had one chasing me last winter. Thought I was gonna die. That's why we like this park. No katts, big or small, are allowed over here."

"We know the rules," said Oscar, his voice cracking a little.

"Huh," said George. "Funny. You don't sound like any lion I've ever met..."

Molly quickly changed the subject back. "Which way did the dogg go?"

"North," said Gertrude. "We watched him head up to that clearing you folks got, near the bend in the river, there."

"Thank you!" said Molly. "Come on, Oscar."

"Oscar?" said George. "I've never heard of a lion named Oscar."

"It's short for Simba," said Oscar, dropping his voice as low as it could go and then growling some.

"Yeah," said Molly. "Come on, Cousin Simba."

They scurried away from the border and made their way into a clearing, a field filled with katt grass.

"It's a special mixture of wheat berry, barley, and rye seeds," explained Molly. "Oh, I'd love to rub my nose on this whole field! Then I'd gobble it down."

"I thought you guys only ate grass when you had a stomachache."

"Urban myth, Oscar." Molly couldn't resist. "Just one rub!" She flopped down in the field and tumbled and somersaulted through the green shoots. "This is better than kattnip!"

"Molly!" said Oscar. "Look!"

He pointed to a rolled-up scroll of parchment that Molly's rolling had just revealed.

"That's Romaldo's love poem!" said Oscar. "The one he wanted me to deliver to Violet!"

Chapter 24

Are you sure that's the same poem?" asked Molly.

Oscar unrolled the scroll.

"Hang on to your stomach," he warned Molly. "If it is, this thing will get sappy and mushy, fast."

Molly moved closer and read over Oscar's shoulder. He cleared his throat and started proclaiming what Romaldo had written.

My dearest Violet
Eyes of gray

Ears of white
Truly
My own
Eyes have never beheld
A beauty
That shines
The way yours doth
Hear my heart
Eagerly beating . . .

"Enough," cried Molly, bringing her paws up to her ears. "How come the sentences are so short? And why are there eleven lines when he could've written all that in one single terrible sentence?"

Oscar shrugged. "That's just what poets do sometimes. I think. I never got my Dogg Scout poetry badge. It has a harp on it."

"Your cousin Romaldo's poem is of absolutely no help to us!" said Molly.

Oscar rerolled the scroll and tucked it into a pocket. "Probably not. But, it proves the giraffes were right. Romaldo was headed this way! He was headed north."

"So let's keep moving north!"

Oscar and Molly hiked across the open field. There was a line of trees about a hundred yards ahead of them and the rippling river to their right.

"Wow," said Oscar. "Look at all that sparkling water."

Molly lowered her head as she walked and seemed to be studying her shoes.

"It's pretty!" said Oscar. "The sun is sending up all sorts of reflections. Check it out, Molly! Reflections are dancing everywhere!"

"I can't," Molly exploded. "If I do, Oscar, I'll get mesmerized. All I'll want to do is chase the tiny dots of light!"

"You mean like those guys?"

Molly raised her eyes an inch or two to see what Oscar was talking about. Twelve tough-looking katts had just burst onto the field to chase shiny flickers of light.

"I got it!" shouted one. "Swatted it good, too!"

"I crushed mine," hollered another. "No. Wait. It got away!"

"I see it!" said the third. "It went that way!

Come back here, you twinkling fairy!"

"Those are alley katts," whispered Molly. "They don't see much sunshine on a regular basis. They're even more nocturnal than most katts."

"Sure," said Oscar. "Because they have to sit on garbage can lids and yowl at the moon all night. I've seen movies."

"So," Molly explained, "when an alley katt experiences the great outdoors for the first time, they go a little bonkers."

"Uh-oh," said Oscar. "Looks like they're bonkers-bouncing this way."

"Hey, youse guys!" shouted one of the alley katts. "It's a lion!"

"No way, Knuckles," said another. "You're lyin'."

"No, Frankie. *He* is."

"Act like a katt, Oscar," coached Molly.

Oscar licked his paws. Repeatedly. He hoped he wouldn't have to lick his belly to prove he was of the feline persuasion.

The seven swaggering katts sauntered over to check out their first real live lion.

"Uh, hi, guys," said Molly. "This is my cousin. Simba. He's here on vacation."

"Hey," said the alley katts.

"Uh, hellooooooooo!" said Oscar, attempting to roar.

"Whoa," said the leader of the alley gang, Knuckles. "You have very meaty breath."

"Thanks."

"So are you two out here searching for the

dogg?" asked Knuckles. "You know, the katt-napper?"

"Uh, yeah," said Molly. "We thought we'd help with the search."

"Well, don't," sneered Knuckles. "Some rich dude named Boomer Hissleton the Third, Esquire just posted a reward for catching and capturing the dirty dogg."

"Excuse me?" peeped Oscar, sounding very un-lionish again.

"A reward, pal. Moola kaboola. Money. Tons of it. And we intend to be the ones enjoying that particular payday."

"We're not interested in the money," said Molly.

"Oh," said Knuckles, turning up his nose. "You're one of those rich katts. Probably have your own bed..."

Molly smiled. She couldn't help it. "Several, actually. I'm Molly Hissleton."

"You related to the rich dude?"

"Oh, yes. He is my father. He gives me money all the time. I don't really need any more of it."

"Riiiiight," said Knuckles, peering at Molly a

little more closely. "You're the katt who wants to be an actress. I recognize them blue eyes and all that fluffy white fur. I seen you on TV back when me and my crew were bunking in that alley behind the TV store. You're the one who made nice with the dogg."

"Well, I wouldn't say we 'made nice.' That implies friendship. We simply survived together in the wilderness."

Oscar probably should've been hurt by Molly's remark. But he was too distracted. And it wasn't because of all the reflected light still bounding and bobbling around the open field.

No, he saw something behind the alley katts. Something hopping from limb to limb up in the trees at the far edge of the meadow.

But then it jumped to the ground.

Because it was a squirrel!

Chapter 25

Squirrel!" Oscar pointed his paw the way his friend Poindexter, who was a pointer, had taught him. "Squirrel! Squirrel! SQUIRREL!"

"Um, settle down, Simba," urged Molly.

But Oscar couldn't settle down, not when he'd just seen a squirrel. Instincts kicked in and his strong, muscular tail wanted to wag so badly, it exploded out of the seat of his pants so it could wiggle freely. It ripped Blaze's borrowed jeans at the seam.

"Hey," said Knuckles. "That ain't no lion's tail."

"Cuz that ain't no lion!" shouted one of his crew. "That's a dogg, Knuckles! A dogg, I tell ya!"

Oscar blasted off because the squirrel was RIGHT THERE! Hopping and prancing in the shadows underneath the trees. Oscar sprinted through the waving field of grain, his tail wagging behind him.

"Simba?" Molly shouted after him. "Distant cousin Simba?"

Molly panicked as Oscar dashed for the tree line.

"Let's go grab that dogg!" shouted Knuckles. "He might be the katt-napper. We can drag him to fluffy fur's daddy and claim the reward!"

The alley katts were about to give chase.

"Wait!" commanded Molly, using the voice she'd use if she ever played a queen onstage. "There's no need to chase after that dastardly dogg. The reward is already yours."

"Huh?"

"Simply tell my father that you successfully chased the katt-napper out of the katt zone and you shall be quite handsomely rewarded for your efforts."

"That'll work? We just collect the cash? We don't actually have to do no chasing?"

"Of course you don't, silly katt. You're on vacation. Why, you haven't even had time to roll in the katt grass or sniff that clump of kattnip I spy over there."

Knuckles's eyeballs bugged out as they zoomed in on the fragrant kattnip just waiting for him.

"Come on, guys," he said. "Let's take time to smell the kattnip. We'll claim the reward later."

The seven alley katts descended on the kattnip. Soon they were giggling and acting goofy, rolling on their backs, playing hide-and-seek with any sparkling reflections that drifted their way.

With any luck, she thought, *they'll get so giddy they'll forget all about the phony lion named Simba and claiming any reward.*

"Ppppprrrrrrrrrr!" She heard Knuckles purr like a motorboat. "Mrrrooowww! I ain't never been so happy! I'm gonna roll around upside down!"

Oh, yeah. A little more kattnip and Knuckles would soon forget all about Simba. He might even forget his own name.

Molly dashed off to the tree line to rejoin Oscar.

As she neared the edge of the woods, she saw the *no trespassing* signs. SQUIRREL ZONE. NO KATTS BEYOND THIS POINT.

And then she heard a steady barrage of pellets pelting the forest floor.

It sounded like a hailstorm.

She also heard Oscar yelping.

"Help! Molly? Squirrel attack!!!"

Chapter 26

Oscar danced a little jig, dodging and ducking, using his front legs to block the acorn attack showering down on his head.

"How dare you!" chittered a squirrel. "What's the matter? Can't you read? You exited the katt zone, Mr. Lion. You exited it big time!"

The shelling stopped long enough for Oscar to tear off his fake lion head.

"I'm not a lion! I'm a dogg!"

The squirrel shrieked in horror. "A dogg?!? That's even worse! Get out of our forest. This land is our land! This land is NOT your land! It's also not somebody's front lawn where you can TER-RORIZE us up a tree!"

The chattering squirrel sounded very, very angry (and a little nutty).

"We're calling Superintendent Bob!" it hollered. "Oh, yes, we are. We're calling him right now! Where's Charlie? CHARLIE?!? Get over here."

Oscar heard a gentle whoosh as a flying squirrel drifted in for a landing in the tree directly overhead. The one where his most annoyed tormentor was perched with an armful of acorns he was ready to rain down on Oscar's noggin.

"Yes, sir, Squiggy?" the flying squirrel said to the one who couldn't fly but could definitely chuck an acorn.

"Swoop over to the park superintendent's gatehouse. Tell that bear we have a trespasser. The worst kind. A dogg!"

"Oh, yeah. I see him down there. Can I spit a nut outta my cheek at him, Squiggy?"

"Knock yourself out."

There was quick *pffft* peashooter sound and

Oscar was beaned on his snout by a very slobbery, half-chewed green acorn. Yuck.

Molly came running over to join Oscar.

"Are you okay?" she asked.

"Yeah. I think so. I have a few bumps on my head and a new one on my nose, but—"

"Another katt?" screamed the squirrel named Squiggy. "First a lion, then a dogg, and now a katt? Could this day get any worse? No, it could not. Fly, Charlie, fly. Alert the park superintendent. We have invaders!"

Charlie took flight.

Squiggy conked Molly on the head with a well-flung walnut. And then the shelling began again in earnest. An army of angry squirrels hurled all sorts of hard-shelled projectiles. Nuts came cascading out of the trees. Pecans, hickory nuts, almonds, hazelnuts, and, of course, acorns.

"We need to exit Nutsville!" shouted Molly.

"I agree! We're on a mission to find our cousins!"

So they ran as fast as they could, deeper into the woods. Where all the trees were filled with

squirrels. Lots and lots of squirrels. All of them squeaking and chittering and flinging even more mixed nuts at Oscar and Molly.

"Pretty soon," said Oscar, between pants for breath, "there's going to be more nuts on the ground than up in the trees!"

"Guess the squirrels are trying to plant themselves a new forest," said Molly sarcastically.

Now Oscar and Molly weren't just getting conked on the head. They also had to contend with running over a rolling sea of slippery shells. It was like trying to jog across a shallow pit filled with wet ping-pong balls.

Finally, they saw the yellow signs posted to tree trunks. The borderline. It was only about one hundred feet away.

"Great!" said Molly. "We make it to the other side of those trees and our troubles are over. No more nutty squirrels!"

"Yeah!" said Oscar eagerly.

Then his nose twitched. Something foul and noxious was tickling it. Something extremely oily and stinky.

"Oh, boy," he moaned.

Oscar knew where they were headed before the next *no trespassing* signs were close enough to read: NO SQUIRRELS ALLOWED. YOU ARE ENTERING THE SKUNK ZONE.

Chapter 27

"Oscar?" groaned Molly as she ran after him, wishing she wasn't *behind* him. "What's that smell? Did you do that?"

"Nope. Read the sign."

"I can't. My katt vision is worse than your dogg vision, remember?"

"Oh, right. Sorry. The only way out of squirrel land is through skunk town!"

"Fine. I'll stop breathing through my nose."

"Good idea," said Oscar.

To avoid smelling skunk, Molly was open-mouth

breathing, which is usually a sign of distress for katts. Well, she was definitely in distress. She had lumps on her head from taking a nut shower. Her nose was under siege from skunk stench. Plus, she was traipsing through parts of the park where she shouldn't set paw. That'll distress a katt.

"Well, hello," hissed a husky voice. It was a skunk, of course. "Thank you so much for attempting to sneak into our territory. We don't get too many intruders. Our scent seems to scare all the other species away. You two must be very brave or very stupid."

"Oh, Bolly's brave," said Oscar. "Trust be. Bravest katt I ever bet."

"Do you always sound like that when you speak, dogg?" sneered the skunk.

"Dope. Just dod't wadt to use by dose whed I talk right dow."

"Be, deither," said Molly.

"Really?" The skunk smiled slyly. "I wonder why?" He sniffed under his armpits. "I know I used deodorant this morning. Well, it doesn't matter. I'm extremely happy to see you two."

"You are?" said Oscar, nervously twitching his tail.

"Oh, yes, indeedy," said the skunk. "For I haven't had any spray practice since I came to the Eastern Wilderness Reserve a week ago."

"Spray practice?" said Molly, arching her eyebrows and forgetting to hold her nose. "Is that like play practice? Because I'm an actress and—"

"This, my dear trespasser, is spray practice!"

The skunk hopped up, spun around, flipped up its tail, and let loose with a misty blast of freshly putrid skunk stench.

"Gotcha!" the skunk shouted with glee. "Oh, yeah. Gotcha good. Hang on. Reloading. Here comes another blast of skunkified gas!"

"Rud!" Molly shouted at Oscar. "This guy sbells worse thad the school cafeteria od beadie weedie wedsday!"

And so Molly and Oscar were once again running through trees, dodging more incoming attacks.

Skunks seemed to be hidden behind every bush, shrub, rock, and tree trunk. They all had their P.U. ready to spew.

"It's id by fur!" wailed Molly. "I'll dever get rid of the sbell."

"Tobato juice," suggested Oscar, between gulps for breath. "Tobato juice will elibidate the sbell."

Fortunately, the skunk zone wasn't very wide or very long. It was conveniently bordered on the north by the binturong zone, a steamy tropical rain forest that was home to shy and shaggy-haired bear cats whose pee smelled like buttered popcorn.

"Yes! I can breathe again!" rejoiced Molly as she and Oscar scampered through the new territory.

"And I want to watch a movie," said Oscar, savoring the buttered popcorn aroma wafting on the breeze. "Maybe that one about the dogg who can dunk basketballs. I like that one."

"Oscar!" said Molly. "Look. Snagged on that shrub."

"The shiny thing?"

"Yes!"

Molly sprang closer to the bush to examine the spangly ornament glued to a gummy leaf.

"This is a sequin from Cousin Violet's necklace!" gushed Molly. "I recognize it. She must've brushed by this shrub on her way to meet your cousin Romaldo. We're on the right track!"

"Woo-hoo," cried Oscar. "Let's celebrate with a big tub of buttered popcorn."

"Oscar?"

"Yes, Molly?"

"You know that what you're smelling is bear cat pee, right?"

"Seriously?"

"Seriously."

"Oh. I did not know that. Forget the celebration. Hold the popcorn. We should forge on. We're on a mission..."

"To save our cousins. So you keep saying."

"And, from all the evidence, we're heading in the right direction!"

But the way forward was blocked.

By a four-wheel-drive vehicle.

Bob the bear was behind the wheel.

Chapter 28

Well, hello, there," he said with a chuckle. "Fancy meeting you two here. A dogg and a katt. Too bad this isn't the dogg section or the katt section."

"We got lost," said Oscar. "Molly and me."

"Together?" said the bear, lifting a single eyebrow in disbelief. "Interesting. But, well, I've been receiving quite a few complaints about you two. Usually, I ignore complaints. But then everybody starts complaining about their complaints not being heard. Today? All the complaints coming in are about you two."

He fished out his phone, which was large, the size of a flat lunch box, because his paws were so huge and clumsy. It made scrolling the screen difficult.

"Let's see." He checked his text messages. "The rhinos. The squirrels. The skunks. Even my buttery popcorn pals the binturong bear cats. Everybody hates you two. Wow. It's hard to upset a bear cat. They're so mellow."

Bob tucked away his phone, shook his head, and rumbled up a belly laugh.

"Sorry," he said. "Just had a flashback to something a lady friend told me back in the day. She was a hippy-dippy polar bear. I dug her. She had beautiful white fur, man. Sort of like yours."

Molly curtsied. "Thank you."

"Her fur stinks like skunk right now," offered Oscar. "But we're gonna fix that with tomato juice. As soon as we find some tomato juice. Is there a tomato zone?"

"Nope," said Bob. "Fruits and vegetables get along just fine. They mix, they mingle. They make beautiful salads together. It's just the creatures we have to keep apart because that's the way of the world. Whole lot of hate goin' on. My polar bear lady friend disagreed. She thought the world would be a better place if we all worked together. Like I said, she was a little wacky."

"Wonder whatever happened to her?" Bob said with a wistful sigh. "Probably grew up, like we all do, and learned the sad, sad truth. In the real world, it's every beast for themselves."

"We're sorry we broke the rules," said Oscar, "but we are on a very important mission. It's urgent, even."

"Is that so?" said the bear, scratching himself. "What's the mission, kid?"

"It's kind of secret," said Oscar.

"Then I 'kind of' need to run you two back to the gatehouse and lock you up till your parents fetch you. Oooh, I bet they're going to *love* hearing about you two, a dogg and a katt, sworn enemies for life, frolicking together through the forest. Again. Oh, yeah. I recognize you two. Molly and Oscar, right? Francine the ferret had you do that show on TV…"

"We were not frolicking!" said Molly, blushing under her facial fur. "We were trying to find my cousin, Violet Hissleton!"

"And *my* cousin," said Oscar. "Romaldo Monta-hugh. We think they're, you know, together."

The bear quit scratching his stomach. "Together? Violet Hissleton and Romaldo Monta-hugh?" He tapped the information into his jumbo phone. "Thank you. I needed their names for my, uh, report…"

"They're in love, okay?" blurted Molly. "That means they might do stupid stuff. Love will do that. Oooh, you made me say the L word. Twice! It's so gross. What's even grosser is the mushy poem Romaldo wrote for Violet."

"It's sappy," said Oscar. "Here. I'll show you."

Oscar unfurled the parchment scroll. He held it out in front of him like it was a stinky pair of socks. The bear leaned in to read it.

My dearest Violet
Eyes of gray
Ears of white
Truly
My own
Eyes have never beheld
A beauty
That shines
The way yours doth
Hear my heart
Eagerly beating

Go where
I
Am
Now and
Together we
Shall
Truly be happy furever.
Once together
Never
Ever
Shall we part

"That's terrible," said Bob.

"We know," said Molly. "So many short, choppy lines. It really disrupts the flow. He'd never make it as a rapper."

"By any chance is this Romaldo Montahugh you're looking for a Dogg Scout?" asked Bob.

"Yes, sir," said Oscar. "But he's not a very good one."

"Well, he sure seems to be working on his secret codes merit badge."

"Maybe. He did send me a letter. The stamp was top secret because..."

Then Oscar finally saw it himself.

"Wowsers! This isn't a poem. It's a secret message."

Chapter 29

What?" said Molly. "What do you two see? What are you gawping at, Oscar?"

"It's a simple first letters code!" Oscar replied. "Duh. I should've seen it the first time I looked at the scroll because I already have my secret codes merit badge. That's why there are so many lines in the poem. So the first letters of each line could spell out a message!"

He handed the scroll to Molly. She read the love poem, fighting the urge to urp up a hair ball, and concentrated on the first letter in every line.

My dearest Violet
Eyes of gray
Ears of white
Truly
My own
Eyes have never beheld
A beauty
That shines
The way yours doth
Hear my heart
Eagerly beating
Go where
I
Am
Now and
Together we
Shall
Truly be happy furever.
Once together
Never
Ever
Shall we part

She put the letters together and broke them up into words. "'Meet me at the Giant Stones'?" she said.

"Yep!" said Oscar. "That's what I got, too."

Molly turned to Bob. "Do you know what it means?"

"Heh-heh-heh," chuckled Bob. "I might."

"You know where Romaldo wanted Violet to meet him, don't you?" said Molly. "You know how to find these Giant Stones!"

"Is there a stone zone?" asked Oscar.

"No. Stones and rocks and pebbles get along just fine. Like I said, it's just the animals we have to worry about." He sighed. "Lion hates zebra, zebra hates lion. Fox hates rabbit, rabbit hates fox. The salmon in the rivers aren't too crazy about me, although I love them. Very tasty..."

Molly didn't want to hear any more about prey and predators. She wanted to find her cousin and bring her back to camp so Violet could marry Phineas Fatt and make Grandma Theodosia happy. If Grandma Theodosia was happy, Molly and her family would stay happy, too. And rich.

So she basically erupted in the bear's face.

"What are these Giant Stones? Where are they?"

Her eruption made Bob blink. "Oh, they're a very famous romantic landmark. Just about a half a mile north of here. On the coast. They jut out into the ocean like a staircase of stepping-stones."

"The ocean was on my grandpa's map!" said Oscar. "There were different zones for fish and dolphins and sharks and..."

"Sea urchins, lobsters, shrimp, jellyfish," said Bob with a heavy sigh. "The ocean is a total zoo. Very fluid boundary lines. Fortunately, it's not my jurisdiction, so it's not my problem. It's Moby's. He's a whale. A great big white thing. Anyway, the Giant Stones are very dramatic, what with the waves crashing against them, the ocean spraying up, and the sunset views up on the top step of the boulder staircase. Lots of weddings take place out there. Very romantic."

"Aha!" said Oscar. "If it's romantic, that's where Romaldo would go. He wears shirts with puffy sleeves."

"Of course, there's a legend about why they're called the Giant Stones," said Bob, leaning casually against his vehicle, like Molly and Oscar had all day to listen to him weave his tales.

"I'm sure it's a very fascinating legend," said Molly. "Gripping, even. And we'd love to hear it. Later. After we find Cousin Violet."

The bear didn't hear a word Molly said. He had a story to tell.

"Millions of years ago," he said, his voice deep and rumbly and mysterious, "back when giants roamed the earth, one from the land on this side of the ocean fell in love with one from the land on the other side. The rock formations along the coast were the giants' stepping-stones so they could visit each other."

"Sweet," said Molly. "Now, where exactly should—"

"But then," said the bear, still oblivious, "others say that the giants weren't in love. Nope. They were fighting each other. They built the stone walkway so they could fight, face-to-face."

"The second legend?" said Bob. "The one where they attack each other? Yeah. That's the one I'd go with."

"Is that the end of your legends?" asked Molly, sounding slightly miffed.

"Yep. Good luck on your quest. When you start smelling the ocean, you'll know you're close."

"You're not going to haul us back to the gatehouse?" said Oscar.

"Nah," said Bob, waddling back to his four-wheel-drive vehicle, hauling himself up, and adjusting his belly so he could squeeze in behind the wheel. "You two little rascals are just trying to do a good deed. Go find your romantic runaway relatives. I'll let it slide this time. Be careful on the hike back, though. Maybe stick to the other side of the river. Don't disturb the same animals on the way back that you bothered on the way up."

"Sounds like a plan," said Oscar. "Thank you, sir."

"Yes," said Molly, softening slightly. "Thank you."

"No problemo. Just keep heading north through the bird zone. And Molly?"

"Yes, sir?"

"No snacking allowed."

Chapter 30

Bob watched the young katt and dogg disappear into the forest.

And then the burly bear dug out his phone again.

He needed to phone a friend. Francine the ferret.

Because Bob had a huge, juicy scoop for her show on the Weasel Broadcasting Network.

Chapter 31

Meanwhile, back in Kattsburgh, the filthy rich Theodosia Hissleton and the even wealthier Phineas Fatt were hosting a small tea party for their one invited guest: Francine, the ferret who worked for the Weasel Broadcasting Network.

Francine wrinkled her nose as she studied the tray of dainty sandwiches with their crusts trimmed off. The ferret was a carnivore. That meant she was supposed to eat meat. There didn't seem to be meat on any of the sandwiches.

"Cream cheese and cucumbers?" she said, looking down her snout in disgust.

"Nyes," said Theodosia.

"I ate all the cookies and scones," said Phineas. "While we were waiting for you to get here." And then he burped.

"How about egg salad?" asked the ferret. "You have any egg salad sandwiches?"

"Ate those, too," said Phineas, with another loud and eggy belch. "Delish."

"Fine. I'll just sip my tea. Do I have to stick out my pinky like that?"

"Oh, nyes," said Theodosia. "Nyes, indeed."

"So, Theodosia?" said the ferret after loudly slurping down some tea. "Give. What's the big news? Is it something for the Weasel Broadcasting Network's high society report?"

Theodosia sat up a little straighter in her chair, presenting herself as an empress on her throne.

"Oh, this is the highest of high society news."

"Good. Gimme, gimme."

"This is an exclusive," Theodosia said conspiratorially. "You and the WBN will be the first to hear this. Ahem." She cleared her throat and sat up even straighter. "Phineas Fatt, the most eligible bachelor in all of Kattsburgh, will soon be engaged to my beautiful granddaughter, the lovely Violet Hissleton. The wedding will—"

The ferret's phone started to buzz and thrum.

"Hold that thought, dearie. I have to take this. It's from my number one talent scout for *Furry Family Feud*. This guy knows how to put together a real kattfight." She brought the phone to her ear. "Talk to me, Bob."

"Hiya, Francine," whispered the bear on the

other end of the call. "Just picked up a little intel. What's it worth to you?"

Francine turned her head to make doubly sure the two katts couldn't eavesdrop on her conversation with Bob, the superintendent of the Eastern Wilderness Reserve.

"Tell me what you've got and I'll tell you what I've got to give," she whispered back.

"Fine. Violet Hissleton and Romaldo Montahugh are a thing. They're in love."

"No!"

"Yes! I think we might be looking at a possible elopement."

"Where can I find them?"

"They're on their way to the Giant Stones. Very romantic. What with the sea spray and whatnot."

The ferret jotted it all down. She then informed Bob that he had earned triple his usual finder's fee.

"Sweet," said Bob.

They ended the call and the ferret's eyes darted back and forth, which is what they always did when she was hatching a scheme.

"Francine?" said Theodosia. "Who was that? What's going on? Your eyes are darting back and forth."

"Oh, it was nothing really. But, well, I do have to look into it. Check it out."

"But what about the Phineas and Violet story?"

"Uh, yeah," said the ferret, sounding even shiftier than usual. "We're gonna need to put a pin in that for a bit. This call was about *Furry Family Feud*. My number one, top-rated game show. It takes priority over everything. Need to hop right on this tip..."

Then inspiration struck.

"But, don't worry, Theodosia. We'll talk. There might be a way to work the Phineas–Violet story into the show."

Theodosia made a face like she'd smelled bad cheese. "A *game* show?"

"That's right. A game show that's watched by millions. Trust me, if Phineas were to declare his love for Violet on this episode I'm dreaming up, it would definitely be the biggest, most sensational, high society story of the year!"

Because, the ferret thought with glee, *Romaldo will be there, too—declaring his love for Violet. I'll set it up as a big surprise. Shock everybody with the news. A Montahugh in love with a Hissleton. The rich kid Phineas Fatt publicly humiliated. Every eyeball throughout the land would be glued to the TV to see that. It'll be a streaming sensation. Furry Family Feud would become a real family feud where the fur would definitely fly!*

If Francine could pull this off, it would become the Weasel Broadcasting Network's biggest smash hit of the year.

Chapter 32

Oscar and Molly hiked through the bird zone—the last restricted area before they'd reach the shore and the Giant Stones.

Birds were chirping and singing in all the trees.

"This is nice," observed Oscar, taking in a deep breath, filling his snout with the sweet scents of the forest. "Nobody trying to chase us out of their zone. Nobody attacking us. Because all the birds are up there, in the trees and the sky and—"

As Oscar pointed up, a gunky white glob splattered him in his right eye.

"I'm glad this isn't the flying cow zone," he whimpered as he wiped the sticky bird poo off his face.

Molly was also gazing up into the trees. Dozens and dozens of birds were sitting in the branches, singing their songs. Building their nests. Fluffing their feathers. A few were in a shallow puddle of water, splashing around, taking a bird bath.

And Molly was drooling.

"Molly?" said Oscar. "Focus. This is not the snack food aisle at the supermarket. This is simply a zone we must cross to reach our ultimate destination: the Giant Stones where we'll find Romaldo and Violet."

"This is so unfair," Molly pouted. "What if we were hiking through the dogg biscuit zone?"

"Um, I don't think crunchy cookies ever come to the Eastern Wilderness Reserve on vacation. They'd get soggy, fast."

"Fine," said Molly. "I'll just close my eyes, shut out all temptation, and follow after you."

"Great. Grab my tail. I'll lead the way."

Molly took the tip of Oscar's tail into her paw and they shuffled forward.

"You know," said Oscar, "we work together pretty good."

"Only because we have to."

"Yeah. I guess so. Although I kind of, sort of enjoy it..."

"Me, too," said Molly. "Temporarily."

"True. Wouldn't want it to become, you know, an everyday thing."

"That would just be weird. Ouch." Molly, with her eyes closed, didn't see the rock waiting to stub her paw.

"Hang on," said Oscar. "I smell something."

"So do I," said Molly. "Probably because I'm holding up your tail and walking behind you."

Oscar's nose started working overtime. He sniffed something. Something important.

"Oscar?" said Molly. "I hear you snorting. What's up?"

"The air! It smells familiar. Cedar and vanilla. Cousin Romaldo! He uses fur moisturizer. Excuse me. I'm on the trail of a smell and I've gotta sniff it."

Oscar dropped down to all fours and, wiggling the wet tip of his nose to open his nostrils wide, started snuffling along the ground.

"Aha!" he said.

"What?" said Molly, both eyes popping open.

"It's Romaldo's phone. It was buried under some leaves."

"What's it doing on the ground?"

"Romaldo has a bad habit of tossing his phone up into the air and doing a happy dance whenever he receives especially good news."

Molly scurried over. "What's the news? What's on the screen?"

"A text message! From *your* cousin, Violet!"

"More secret code?"

"Nope. Your cousin is direct and to the point. It just says, 'Meet me at the Giant Stones. They're super romantically awesome.'"

"They both had the same idea," said Molly. "About the Giant Stones."

"Yeah," said Oscar. "Maybe they really do belong together."

"No way," said Molly. "Violet needs to marry Phineas Fatt."

"How come?"

"So I can go to acting school!"

"Oh. Okay."

Molly clasped her paws behind her back and paced. "We have to find them, Oscar. We need to figure this out, like a detective would in a movie. What do we know so far?"

"Well," said Oscar, "Romaldo came to your camp. Because that's where we found his love poem."

"Yes!" said Molly. "He peeked through the window of our camper. Violet wasn't where she was supposed to be. Despondent, Romaldo dropped his coded love poem, which he had hoped to slip through the window to Violet..."

Oscar picked up the thread. "Sad, he moped away. He passed by the giraffes and headed north."

"Why?" said Molly.

"Hang on," said Oscar. He dragged the tip of his paw up the screen of Romaldo's phone to scroll to an earlier message. "Aha. Violet sent him an earlier text!"

"What's it say?"

"'Head north.'"

"That's it?"

Oscar shrugged. "Maybe she'd almost maxed out her monthly data plan."

Molly nodded. "She is on her phone all the time."

"Okay, so Romaldo did as he was instructed. And then, boom—Violet's next text tells him exactly where to go. He tosses his phone into the air, does his happy dance, and dashes off to the Giant Stones."

"Which is exactly what we should do!" said Molly.

"Um, can you dash with your eyes closed?" asked Oscar.

"No. But I promise not to snack on any birds we pass along the way. Come on. It's not too much farther to the ocean. I can smell it."

Oscar smelled it, too. Salty air. That fresh seaside odor.

"Woof-hoo!" he shouted. "Let's hit the beach."

They started running through a clearing.

Which was probably a mistake.

Their burst of motion caught the eye of an eagle circling overhead.

A eagle who liked to snack on kitty-katts. Especially ones who'd wandered into the wrong section of the wilderness.

Chapter 33

Molly saw the widening shadow of a feathery wingspan before she saw the swooping eagle.

It was big and getting bigger because the eagle was close and diving closer.

"This is so unfair, Oscar!" she shouted. "I was eagle-napped the last time we did something dumb together! It's your turn."

"Sorry!" said Oscar as they tried to outrun the looming shadow. "But I think he only has eagle eyes for you."

This can't be happening again! thought Molly.

I'm an actress! I deserve NEW drama!

When Molly and Oscar were lost together (the first time), Molly was plucked out of the back of a weaselboar's truck barreling down a mountain (it's a long story) by a katt-plundering eagle. Oscar had saved one of her nine lives that time. This time? They may not be so lucky.

"You have illegally entered the bird zone, trespasser!" bellowed the very officious-sounding eagle.

"Oscar!" Molly shrieked. She could feel the eagle sink its hooked talons into the scruff of her neck like she was a fluffy prize in a claw game at an arcade.

Oscar spun around and leapt up as high as he could to snap at the eagle. But he couldn't jump high enough. All he bit were a few tail feathers.

The eagle soared skyward, towing Molly up over the treetops toward the clouds.

"Sorry, Molly!" she heard Oscar shout from down below. "But if he drops you, I'll catch you! I promise!"

It was like Molly was on an elevator, but without buttons or even an elevator car. They climbed higher and higher. The eagle piped its high-pitched whistle. For such a big and powerful bird, its call was kind of weak. Almost like a mouse.

"Seriously?" Molly scoffed at her tormentor. "That's all you've got? You whistle like a wheezing rodent. Where's your squawk and squeal?"

"Silence, please," said the haughty eagle. "Show some respect. My relatives are on coins and the tippy tops of flagpoles."

"Doesn't mean you get to turn me into dinner, baldy!"

Molly's shouts only made the eagle tighten its grip on her fur.

Just then, a pair of blue jays zoomed across the sky like supersonic jets.

"Drop the katt, pal!" screeched one of the blue jays.

"Never!" said the eagle. "For I am the most noble bird of all, a bald eagle!"

"So go buy a wig," snickered the other blue jay.

"You tell him, Bernice!" said the first soaring attacker.

"Oh, you bet I will, Bernie. I'll tell him good."

"Are you two attempting to mob me?" sputtered the eagle, sounding a little less valiant and heroic. Molly could feel his talons loosening just a bit. "Are there, by any chance, other members of your extended family flying nearby?"

Bernice soared in, feigning an attack. She spun into a barrel roll and wheeled skyward, squawking. "Eee-eee-eee!"

"Bernice just sent up a mob call, pal," said Bernie. "There's a whole squadron of bad-attitude blue jays just like us ready to pounce. Prepare to be mobbed, chrome dome."

Molly knew from her nature studies class at school that "mobbing" was a defensive tactic used by some species. They worked together to attack and harass a predator. To scare it away!

But now these birds (the sworn enemies of katts) were doing it to protect her.

"Thank you!" she shouted to the blue jays, who kept dive-bombing the eagle. "Thank you, thank you, thank you!"

"Thanks for not nibbling our neighbors," said Bernie, swooping past.

"Not many katts would be so polite," added Bernice on a fly-by.

"How dare you two mob me!" thundered the eagle as he tried to evade the pair of attacking blue jays by nose-diving swiftly toward the ground.

He was plummeting so fast, dragging Molly along for the ride, that her stomach lurched up into her throat while her cheeks fluttered in the breeze.

But she could see Oscar. Down on the ground. Running around and around in circles with his arms open wide.

"You can just drop me off here, sir!" Molly shouted.

The eagle hesitated.

Until he heard a whole chorus of squawking *Eee-eee-eee*s gunning for him.

"Sounds like you've got a whole *mob* of company dropping in!" cracked Molly.

The eagle snapped open his hooked claws.

Molly fell like a fluffy rock, her fur flapping.

She was dropping fast.

Twenty yards from the ground.

Ten.

Five.

PLOP!

She made a soft landing, right in Oscar's arms.

Chapter 34

I thought you were a goner!" Oscar told Molly as he gently lowered her to the ground.

"Yeah," she said. "Me, too. Thank you, Oscar."

"Hey, it's like I said—we're a team. Kind of, sort of."

Molly nodded. "Temporarily."

"So are we!" brayed a voice on a tree branch overhead. It was Bernie, the blue jay. "Only we ain't temporary. This is just how we fly."

"We've been together for years!" added his partner, Bernice.

Bernie shrugged. "Hey, we're blue jays. We find someone we like, we stick with 'em."

"Forever," added Bernice. "Two are better than one."

"Just watch," said Bernie. "Hey, Bernice—why does a flamingo lift up one leg?"

"Because," said Bernice, "if it lifted both legs, it would fall over!"

The two birds laughed at their own joke and slapped their wing tips in a feathery high five.

"See?" said Bernie. "Without Bernice, I'm just a setup without a punch line. A zig without a zag."

Oscar cleared his throat, hoping to quiet the two chattering lovebirds. "Thank you both for saving my friend, Molly."

"Yes, thank you," said Molly. "How can I ever repay you?"

The two birds didn't answer. They looked at each other. They looked back down at Oscar and Molly.

"Seriously?" said Bernie. "You two are friends? A dogg and a katt?"

"Kind of, sort of," said Oscar.

"Temporarily," added Molly.

"Just like how you two broke the rules and befriended a katt!" said Oscar.

"Yeah," said Bernie, looking around nervously. "Don't be spreadin' that around."

"We just don't like bullies," said Bernice. "That eagle? Thinks he's hot stuff. Always wanting to show you the carvings of his 'noble ancestors' on coins and whatnot..."

"And there's more like him in the zone," said Bernie with a beak nod to the sky. "All sorts of birds of prey swooping around up there. We're talking eagles, hawks, falcons...those other things."

"The osprey?" said Oscar.

"Gesundheit," said Bernice and Bernie.

"We're only passing through," said Oscar. "Sorry for the inconvenience."

"Where are you headed?" asked Bernie.

"The Giant Stones," said Molly. "Along the coast."

"Our cousins are there," added Oscar. "We hope."

"Hang on," said Bernie. "We'll drone it for you."

"Huh?" said Oscar.

Bernice shrugged her wing flaps. "We'll fly up a few hundred feet, hover around, see what we can see."

"In case you didn't notice, we've got a special talent," said Bernie. "We can fly. You two can't."

And with that, the two blue jays fluttered up and hovered above the treetops.

"Oooh," said Bernie, who was looking south. "There's a nasty storm brewing. The approaching frontal system may impact any outdoor plans you had for the rest of today. Watch out for thunderboomers and be sure you pack your rain cane."

"Poor Bernie," sighed Bernice. "Always wanted to do the weather on TV. Now here's some news you can use. This just in from the north. There is a teenage dogg and a teenage katt holding paws on the rocks about two hundred yards ahead."

"Oh, yeah," said Bernie, treading air and turning around to see what Bernice had seen. "Very lovey-dovey and romantical, what with the ocean crashing against the stones and spraying up and all."

"The boy is named Romaldo," Bernice shouted down to the ground. "The girl is Violet."

Oscar wagged his tail. "Are you sure?" he called up to the birds.

"Very," said Bernice. "They keep repeating each other's names over and over between smooches."

"Gross," muttered Molly.

"Totally," agreed Oscar. "But, let's go rescue them anyhow."

"Fine," said Molly. "I'll try not to hurl!"

Oscar waved good-bye to the two blue birds. "Thanks again, Bernie and Bernice."

"Happy to help," said Bernie.

"We love seeing couples falling in love," said Bernice.

"They said the L word," muttered Molly.

"Wooooof." Oscar shivered, the way you do when you see a spider.

And then they took off running the final two hundred yards to the rocky shore.

Chapter 35

Molly ran a little faster than Oscar.

Because she didn't want some other bird snagging her coat and taking her home for dinner.

Bird dinner.

They came out of the woods to a flat, stony plane—passing a sign alerting them that they were now under the rules and regulations of the Underwater Ocean Administration. In other words, they were no longer officially in the Eastern Wilderness Reserve. For land creatures like Oscar and Molly, the seaside cliffs and rocks were a no-one's-zone. Molly wondered if that meant the shore belonged to them all.

If so, word hadn't gotten out. The flat gray plane of stone, leading to a jagged bluff, was deserted. Molly still hadn't seen her cousin Violet or Oscar's cousin Romaldo. But she could see the ocean. It was choppy and stretching to the horizon.

Oscar was furiously sniffing the air. "All I'm picking up is salt water and sea breeze. And fish. There're definitely all sorts of fishy smells."

The clouds overhead turned angry and dark. They billowed up into swollen thunderheads and blocked out the sun.

"Oh, tuna treats in my teeth," muttered Molly as a few raindrops began to fall. "I hate the rain."

More droplets pitter-pattered on her head. She rolled her eyes. Rain was sooooo obnoxious.

"If I get wet, I can just shake it off," said Oscar. "Want to see?"

Molly was about to scream *No!* when her phone started chirping (she had a birdsong ringtone) and Oscar's started barking (apparently, he stuck with the default dogg ringtone).

Molly answered her phone. Oscar answered his.

They both drifted away from each other so they could converse in private with whomever was calling. Molly was right at the edge of the cliff.

"Hellooooo?" Molly purred into the phone.

"Molly dear?"

It was her father.

"Why haven't you been answering your phone, darling daughter?"

Funny. Molly's phone hadn't been ringing. Maybe katt phones were blocked in all the non-katt zones she and Oscar had been trespassing through. Now that they were outside the Eastern Wilderness Reserve borders, they had strong signals again.

"I guess I was in a dead zone, Daddy," Molly said with a nervous giggle. Her nerves also made her bounce up on her paws. As she did, she looked down at the ocean.

And saw Violet and Romaldo, locked in a dramatic embrace as the sea spray splashed up around them on the Giant Stones.

"But it was worth the trek! We've found Cousin Violet!"

"We???" said her father.

"I mean, I found her. I said we because, one day, I might want to be a queen. Anyhow, I see Violet and I will now bring her back."

"Where is she?"

"Close to where I am."

"And where, pray tell, are you?"

"Near where Violet is."

"Molly?" Her father was using his stern I'm-not-fooling-around-young-lady voice.

"She's at the shore, okay? Violet's standing on some rocks looking longingly at the crashing ocean. Maybe she left camp because she had a craving for fish that didn't come in a tin can."

"Any sign of a dogg?"

Molly closed her eyes. She hated lying to her father but, right now, it felt like her only choice.

"No," she said. "No doggs."

"Thanks heavens for that!" Molly heard a rustle of paw pads as her father covered his phone and said to someone close by, "Molly has found Violet.

197

Hurrah! Apparently, our darling niece wasn't katt-napped; she simply wandered off to go deep-sea fishing and—"

"Give me that phone, Boomer," snapped an angry voice.

Molly's grandmother.

"Molly," she decreed.

"Yes, Grandmama?" said Molly. She instinctively dipped into a polite curtsy, even though her grandmother couldn't see it.

"You are to haul your cousin back to your campground, immediately. Once Violet marries Phineas Fatt, we Hissletons will have more than enough money to send you to the finest acting school in all the land. Or, if this assignment is too much for you, dear, simply let me know where precisely we might find Violet. I will hire a professional rescue party to retrieve her and, should they so desire, *they* shall be the ones going to the finest acting school in all the land."

Now the rain was really starting to fall. Molly stood there, with a phone glued to one ear, listening to her grandmother threatening to crush her dreams while, simultaneously, getting soaked. This might just be the worst day of her life.

"Don't worry, Grandmama!" she said. "I'm all over it."

Just like the rain is all over me.

Molly ended the call. Now all she had to do was scamper down the staircase of giant stone steps, grab Violet, and haul her back through all those different zones in a torrential downpour while hopefully avoiding eagles, skunks, and nut-chucking squirrels.

Yep.

This was definitely the worst day of her life.

Chapter 36

Meanwhile, in the dogg zone, the Montahugh family gathered for shelter from the storm inside the covered picnic pavilion.

Duke folded his flip phone.

"Good news, everybody," he hollered. "Just got off the horn with Oscar. Seems my Dogg Scout son used his Dogg Scouty skills and tracked down that other Dogg Scout, Romaldo. That's why he wasn't answering his phone. He was too busy sniffing dirt."

"Where is Romaldo?" snapped Grandpa Max.

"Over by the shore. Reckon Romaldo had a hankering for clams or somethin'. Wandered off to get himself a mess of shellfish. Anyhoo, Oscar will be bringing him back, ASAP."

"Good," grumbled Grandpa Max. "Now it's time to choose teams for capture and chew the flag..."

"Excuse me," hissed a voice approaching the pavilion.

"Duke?" said Oscar's mother, Lola. "That looks like that ferret from the Weasel Broadcasting Network. The one who put Oscar on TV with that k-a-t-t."

"Really?" said Duke. "'Cause I don't remember that ferret looking like a soggy fleece squeaky toy someone dropped in a bucket of water."

"Because," snipped the ferret, "the last time we met I wasn't drenched with rain."

"Daddy?" said Oscar's sister, Fifi. "Isn't she, like, a ferret?"

"Yes, dear. That's why your momma and me

called her a ferret instead of, you know, a badger or a porcupine."

"Well," huffed Fifi, "ferrets aren't allowed in the dogg zone."

"That's the dang truth," snarled Grandpa Max. "She belongs with her own kind. The weasels and otters."

Francine the ferret jammed a paw against her hip. "I am neither a weasel nor an otter, sir."

"It don't matter," bellowed Bob the bear, waddling up the trail behind the ferret. "Francine here is with me. On semiofficial business. Means she has a waiver and can enter zones where, otherwise, she would not be authorized to so enter."

"So what do you two want with us?" demanded Oscar's father.

"I heard you discussing a game," said the ferret, slyly wiggling her eyebrows. "Capture and chew the flag, I believe? How would you like to play a game that could make the Montahughs famous throughout the land?"

"You want us to be on television?" grumbled Oscar's father. "Again?"

"She sure does," said Bob the bear.

"Only this time," said the ferret, "you will be the stars. Not Oscar. The whole Montahugh family will be contestants on my game show! Well, your top five players. We can't put *all* of you on TV. You wouldn't fit."

"Are there, like, prizes and stuff?" asked Fifi.

"Oh, yes. Big prizes. Plus, as I said, you'll be famous. Competing on the number one game show of all time, the one that everybody watches: *Furry Family Feud!*"

"*Furry Family Feud?*" said Grandpa Max. "I've seen that show. Usually it's foxes versus rabbits or birds versus insects."

"Yes," said the ferret. "We had to use teeny, tiny microphones for that episode."

"So who'd we be up against?" asked Duke. "Squirrels? Katts?"

"Bingo," said Bob. "You'd be playing against a katt family."

"But not just any katt family," said Francine the ferret. "You'll be going up against...the Hissletons!"

"The Hissletons?" snarled all three dozen doggs.

"We already have a feud with them!" snapped Grandpa Max.

"I know," said the ferret. "And this is your

chance to win it. In public. In front of millions!"

Yep, thought Bob the bear. *And that game show's gonna get even more exciting when Francine reveals her two secret contestants: Romaldo Montahugh and Violet Hissleton.*

Chapter 37

"Come on, Molly!" cried Oscar, bounding across the slick stone plateau leading to the cliff. "They're down below!"

"Can we wait until it stops raining?" asked Molly, who looked absolutely miserable.

"I don't think we can wait that long," said Oscar, studying the dark clouds overhead. "This is going to be a real fur soaker. A gully washer. A poop floater. A sizzly sod soaker."

"Can't you just say it's raining katts and doggs?" said Molly, coming to Oscar's side.

"Oooh," said Oscar with a full-body shudder. "I hate that expression. All I see are doggs and katts tumbling out of the sky and lots and lots of broken legs."

They stood on the ledge of the cliff and peered down.

A series of stepping-stones resembling a giant staircase led all the way down to the ocean where waves crashed against the cubes lining the water's edge. Each wave sent up sheets of foam and sea spray.

Romaldo and Violet were standing at the very bottom of the stone staircase—the last step before they'd wind up in the ocean. They were being drenched by the rain and the constantly crashing waves.

They were also hugging.

"Gross," said Molly.

"Totally," said Oscar. "And soggy, too. Their fur may never dry."

"Well," said Molly with a resigned sigh, "let's climb down and tell them it's time to head home."

"Think they'll listen to us?" asked Oscar.

"Probably not. They're teenagers. But..." Molly held up her phone and wiggle-waggled it. "Violet will listen to our grandmama. She scares everybody."

"Good idea," said Oscar, tapping his phone. "Maybe my grandpa Max can scare Romaldo into coming back to camp. He scares everybody, too."

Oscar began a very careful descent on the first of the steep stones leading down to the ocean. "Follow me," he said to Molly over his shoulder. "And remember to follow the Dogg Scout Three-Point Rule!"

Molly was confused. "You mean from basketball?"

"No. To avoid slipping or falling while climbing up or down anything, always make sure you keep three points of contact. Only move one limb at a time. You should only break the three points of contact when you reach some place with stable footing."

"You mean like a warm and cozy spa? My fur needs a blowout!"

Chapter 38

Finally, after much slow and steady descending, Oscar and Molly reached the stone next to the one their cousins were sharing.

The waves kept crashing. The spray kept spraying. The rain kept slashing. And everybody kept getting wetter and wetter.

"Ewww," moaned Molly. "I smell like the ocean. The stinky parts."

Oscar cupped his hands over his snout and shouted, "Romaldo? Woof-hoo! Ro-mal-do-oh!"

Molly just chucked a sea pebble at Violet.

"Ow-wee," said Violet.

"Are you all right, my love, my turtledove?" gushed Romaldo.

"Nuh-uh. Are there, like, pebbles in the waves? Because the mean old ocean just beaned me."

"That was me, Violet!" shouted Molly. "Over here. Woo-hoo!"

"Turn around, Romaldo," urged Oscar. "Woof-hoo!"

He and Molly were both windmilling their arms over their heads and whistling loudly.

At last, Romaldo and Violet turned around.

"Cousin Oscar?" said Romaldo.

"Cousin Molly?" said Violet.

"Guilty as charged," snipped Molly. She was soooo over this rescue mission in the driving rain. "Come on. We have to head back."

"Excuse me?" said Violet.

"We need to be back at Camp Hissleton. Otherwise Grandmama Theodosia will be furious."

"Who cares?" said Violet. "She's such a party pooper. I'm in love, Molly. Love."

Molly urped. "Excuse me. You're making me seasick."

"You have to leave here, too," Oscar told Romaldo. "The whole family is worried about you."

"Why?" proclaimed Romaldo. "For I, like fair Violet, am in love. And I owe it all to you, Oscar."

"Huh?"

"If you hadn't refused to deliver my love poem, I never would've found the courage to make the journey myself. To climb every mountain and ford every stream until I found my dream."

Oscar exchanged a glance with Molly. Grossed out, they were both a little green around the gills. It didn't matter. All that mattered was Oscar taking Romaldo back to the Montahugh family camp. Molly would do the same with Violet, escorting her back to the Hissleton campsite.

"You guys have to come with us," said Oscar.

"No," said Romaldo. "All we have to do is listen to our hearts."

"Does it say dum-dum-dum, dum-dum-dum?" asked Molly sarcastically. "Because that's how you're behaving. Dumb, dumb, dumb."

"Chill, Molly," said Violet. "One day, when you're older, you'll fall in love, too."

A huge wave slammed into the stones and sent up a wall of water.

"Right now," sputtered Molly, when the wave receded and she was spitting out seaweed, "I just don't want to fall into the ocean."

"Okay," said Oscar. "You leave me no choice, Romaldo. A Dogg Scout is obedient. I have to obey Grandpa Max."

He whipped out his phone.

"And I'm calling Grandmama," fumed Molly, jabbing her paws on the slippery glass face of her wet phone.

"Maybe they can talk some sense into you two!" said Oscar.

"I found her, Grandmama!" Molly said to her phone. "Hold on. Here's Violet."

"Hang on, Grandpa," Oscar said into his. "You can scream all that at Romaldo. He's right here."

Oscar and Molly both held out their phones.

Violet and Romaldo gazed into each other's eyes and nodded, solemnly.

They each took a phone.

And flung both into the ocean.

Chapter 39

You threw my phone into the ocean?" shrieked Molly. "Hello? All my contacts and texts and photos and dramatic monologues were on that phone! You threw away my whole life!"

Romaldo struck a dramatic pose. "Love looks not—"

"Don't you dare try to poem me right now!" screamed Molly. "That. Was. My. Phone!"

"You flung mine into the ocean, too," said Oscar, shaking his head. "That was dumb. Stupid, even. There's a storm blowing through the whole wilderness reserve. We may not survive without real-time weather updates and GPS mapping."

"Um, not to be harsh," said Violet. "But you two sound like old people. Let's dial down the maturity level, okay?"

"You should listen to them!" Bernie the blue jay squawked at Violet.

He and Bernice were battling the blowing wind, bobbing up and down in the air.

"Breaking news!" shrieked Bernice.

"We're tracking the storm with our eyes in the sky," said Bernie. "Right now, an area of high energy is gaining intensity and becoming a spinning pocket of instability. We could be looking at another Big Wind like the record breaker that barreled through here thirty-seven years ago."

"Oh, yeah," said Bernice. "My grandpa told me about that one." She whistled. "The feathers were flying that day."

"Like sticking your face in a blow-dryer," said Bernie. "With the steady rain and thunder boomers, the river breached its banks. Lots of families

216

on both sides had someone swept away in the flood that dreadful day."

Now Violet looked nervous. "They died?"

Bernie and Bernice nodded solemnly.

"Oh, my," gasped Violet. "This is horrible. We should call for help, Romaldo."

"Good idea," he said, clutching her paws in his. "Unfortunately, I tossed away my phone when I jumped for joy after receiving your 'Head north' text."

"And my phone got shattered when all those squirrels in the squirrel zone chucked walnuts at me and I used it as a shield."

"And, then," said Molly, still furious, "you two threw our phones INTO THE OCEAN!"

Violet tried to look cute. She widened her eyes and fluttered her lashes. "Oopsie. Sorry."

"To err is canine," proclaimed Romaldo, "to forgive—"

He wasn't able to complete that particular bit of verse.

"Yikes!" screeched Bernie and Bernice as they

beat their wings into blurs and helicoptered up as far and as fast as they could. "Tsunami!"

A towering wave, taller than the giraffes Molly and Oscar had met earlier, slammed into the giant stone staircase, plunging the first five steps underwater. The katts and doggs were swept under into the strangely silent and murky saltwater darkness.

Molly wondered if she and Violet really did have nine lives like everybody said.

Because she was pretty sure they were both about to lose one.

Chapter 40

At that very same moment, Molly's family was huddled inside their rattling recreational vehicle as its aluminum sides were battered by the sideways slashing rain.

The RV rocked in the unrelenting gusts of wind.

"Do something, Boomer!" commanded Grandmama Theodosia. "Make it stop!"

"Unfortunately, Mommy dearest," replied Molly's father, "although everyone complains about the weather, none of us can do anything about it."

"Unacceptable answer, Boomer! Completely, one-hundred-percent unacceptable!"

Suddenly, there came a rapping of tiny knuckles on the RV's thin metal door.

"Are we expecting company?" asked Molly's mother.

"Heavens no," said Molly's father.

"Unless," said her brother, Blaze, "it's, like, you know, Molly and Violet."

"Impossible. We just finished chatting with your sister. She was at the seashore."

"So? She could've already made it back here if she has, like, a jet pack. And, if she does have a jet pack? I am so totally jealous. I also so totally want a jet pack."

Molly's father rolled his eyes and went to the door to peer out the window.

"It's that filthy ferret," he muttered out of the side of his snout. "And that even grubbier bear."

"The park ranger?" whispered Molly's mother disgustedly.

"Superintendent," growled the bear on the other side of the door. "I am not a ranger, I am a superintendent. Means I'm in charge. I also have very good ears and this door is made out of very thin aluminum. So open it. The water's up to my ankles and the ferret's knees. Our paws are getting moist and mushy out here!"

Reluctantly, Molly's father opened the door. The waterlogged ferret scampered into the trailer. The bear lumbered up the steps behind her, making the RV teeter on its wheels.

"Anybody got a towel?" asked the ferret. "I'm soaked."

Molly's mother handed her a dishrag.

"I'm good," said the bear. "I'll just shake it off."

"Nooooo!" screamed all the katts.

But they were too late. They were pelted by water drops flinging off the bear's jiggly fur in every direction.

"Ew," said Blaze, wiping off the muddy splatter. "You, like, totally brought the rainstorm inside, dude."

"To what do we owe the displeasure of this rude interruption?" demanded Theodosia.

The ferret smiled slyly at her. "Didn't realize you'd left Kattsburgh, Theodosia."

"If you must know, Francine, I came to this dreadful wilderness the moment I heard my darling granddaughter had gone missing."

"Sorry, Momsy," said Mr. Hissleton. "I didn't want to bother you with sad news until I could turn that frown upside down. Rest assured, Violet will soon return. All will be as it should."

"That is so wonderful to hear," said Francine, with a wink to the bear, who seemed to be stifling a chuckle. "And that's the reason for my 'rude interruption,' as you called it. After our delightful tea, I had a brainstorm. I want you folks, the Hissletons, to star on my game show, *Furry Family Feud*. Phineas Fatt will also join you. Before the game begins, Phineas will propose to Violet in front of our TV audience of millions. You want to be the biggest high society news of the season? Maybe even the decade? This is how you do it, Theodosia."

Theodosia crinkled her nose in disgust. "By appearing on a TV game show?"

"Exactly! I'll go pick up Violet in the WBN traffic helicopter. We'll whisk her to a special VIP tent where my crew will give her the glam treatment. Do her wardrobe, fur, and makeup—turn her into a fabulous princess."

"Can't she come home first?" asked Theodosia.

"Oh, no. It's better if we keep her entrance and her glamorous new look a surprise. Because the show is live, darling. We'll want to see the look on all your faces when we make the big reveal. Then, right before the game begins, Phineas proposes to her…"

The bear snorted back a laugh.

"Sorry," he said. "Katt allergies."

"Wipe your nose on your arm," said the ferret. "Where was I?"

Molly's father smiled and tried to help out. "I believe the wealthiest katt in all the land was about to propose to our niece in front of a national television audience after she's surprised us with her glamorous new look?"

"Exactly," said the ferret. "Once he does, we can say he's a member of your family and Phineas can play for your team."

"I like it," said Molly's father. "Heavens, I love it. Momsy? What say you?"

"It's a good plan," agreed Theodosia. "Phineas wouldn't dare back out of a marriage proposal made in front of millions on national TV. Our future is secure. Where and when is this game, Francine?"

"Tomorrow," said the ferret. "Eleven a.m. We broadcast the show live from the Wilderness Reserve welcome center."

"You mean that smelly guard shack we passed on the way in?" asked Blaze.

"Hey," said Bob the bear. "That's *my* smelly guard shack. Those smells are all mine. Plus, it has electricity. For the lights and cameras."

"We'll make it look nice," Francine assured the katts. "Once this storm blows through."

"Might I inquire whom we Hissletons will be competing against?" asked Molly's father eagerly.

The ferret's grin widened. "Why, a dogg family, of course. I believe we have one all lined up." She pretended to be checking notes on her phone. "Oh, yes. Here we are. The Montahughs."

225

Chapter 41

The Montahughs?" gasped all the katts in the RV.

"We already have a feud with them!" hissed Theodosia.

"I know," said the ferret. "And this is your chance to finally win it. In public. In front of millions!"

Bob the bear was loving this. Things hadn't been this exciting in the Eastern Wilderness Reserve in a long time!

Theodosia narrowed her eyes and thought

about it for five full seconds. "Fine," she said. "We'll do it."

Oh, boy, thought Bob the bear. *This is gonna be good!*

He was so excited about the big blowup to come because he knew the truth. Phineas Fatt might be there for the big TV game show but the only proposal would be the one the ferret orchestrated between Romaldo the dogg and Violet the katt.

The Hissletons and Montahughs would go to war!

Live, on national TV!

He needed to race over to the Western Frontier Park, find his old hippy-dippy polar bear lady friend, and give her a front row seat to the bare-clawed battle. He wanted her to see these two families tear each other apart. He'd show her once and for all that he was right and she was wrong.

Sworn enemies for life could never, *ever* find a way to just get along.

Chapter 42

Holding his breath, Oscar scissor-kicked to where Romaldo was attempting to rescue Violet.

Unfortunately, Romaldo wasn't a very good swimmer.

Guess he never earned THAT merit badge, thought Oscar.

Molly, her cheeks ballooning with her last deep breath, shot over to help, because Romaldo was all tangled up in his puffy shirt. The billowy sleeves had become snagged on a barnacle-encrusted chunk of coral.

Oscar grabbed Violet by the scruff of her neck. Molly slashed a gash in the cuff of Romaldo's fancy pirate shirt, freeing him from the coral.

Then Oscar and Molly dragged Violet and Romaldo up to the surface, where all four gasped for a fresh breath of air, bobbing up and down in the choppy, cresting waves.

"Okay," shouted Oscar. He had to shout to be heard over the crashing waves and raging storm. "We're gonna be okay. Everybody take a deep breath and then start swimming for the rocks."

But they didn't have to swim.

A curling wave came along, lifted them up about ten feet, and hurled them to the shore with its surf.

"Grab something and hold on!" Oscar cried out as the wave began its foamy retreat to the sea.

He helped Violet hook on to a stepping-stone and grabbed one himself. Molly was doing the same with Romaldo. Violet and Romaldo might've been teenagers, both of them older than Molly and Oscar, but they were very babyish when it came to important stuff like "How to Not Panic and Stay Alive."

"Ohmigosh," burbled Violet, spitting out seawater, panting breathlessly. "That was horrible. I chipped a claw on the coral."

"At least we're alive!" said Molly. "Because Oscar saved you while I saved Romaldo."

"How can I ever repay you?" Romaldo gushed, picking at the seaweed clinging to the sleeve of his puffy shirt. He examined the spot where Molly had sliced through the fabric. "And did you, by any chance, bring along a sewing kit?"

"No!" said Oscar. "She did not. But she did save your life."

"Yeah," said Molly. "It's amazing what katts and doggs can do for each other when they're not fighting like katts and doggs!"

They slowly made their way up the stone staircase, ahead of the next crashing wave.

"I love katts," said Romaldo, batting his eyelashes, reaching out to take Violet's paw as they climbed. "Well, one katt in particular."

"Meeyowzer," purred Violet, puckering up for a smooch.

They both raised two arms, about to swoon into a hug.

"Three-point rule!" Oscar shouted. "Three-point rule!!! When climbing slippery rocks, always keep three limbs in contact with a surface at all times."

"And no more mushy stuff," added Molly. "There's only so much our stomachs can take!"

Chapter 43

The four climbers clambered up and over the ledge and stood on the cliff.

The rain had stopped but the winds were swirling fiercely, creating small typhoon funnel clouds wherever they sucked up a rain puddle.

"We need to get you two back to camp," said Molly, shouting over the blustery gusts. "Now!"

"And," said Oscar, "we need to hike back on the *eastern* shore of the river."

"Why, pray tell?" asked Romaldo.

"Because," said Molly, "we came up on the

western side. Let's just say we've already worn out our welcome over there."

"I'm hungry," whined Violet.

"What?" said Romaldo, straining to hear Violet's whimper over the whistling of the wind.

"I need a snack or I'm going to turn hangry. That's hungry and angry!"

"I'm afraid I didn't pack any snack food items," said Romaldo, patting all his pockets. "Except, of course, breath mints. But perhaps I could scurry back down to the ocean and grab you a fresh fish?"

"No!" Oscar and Molly shouted together.

"You're not scurrying back to the ocean!" said Molly.

"I don't like fish," pouted Violet.

And I bet they're not too crazy about you, was what Oscar wanted to say, but he bit his tongue. Ouch. That hurt.

"There's plenty of food back at our campground," Oscar reminded Romaldo.

"And we have all sorts of snacks stashed in the cupboards of the RV," Molly said to Violet.

Violet stomped her feet in a puddle. "But, I'm hangry now!"

"Don't look at us," chirped a pair of voices overhead. It was Bernie and Bernice. The blue jays.

"We have to take off," said Bernice.

"Too much turbulence in the air," added Bernie. "Winds are still gusting up to forty miles per hour."

"We wish we could guide you home," said Bernice.

"But," said Bernie, "we should really stick to our own zone."

"However, if there's an emergency," said Bernice.

"Just give us a call," said Bernie. "A bird call!"

And then, together, they both laughed. "Eee-eee-eee!"

"Which zone is next on this side?" Oscar shouted up at the two birds flapping hard to stay aloft in the blowing wind.

"Looks like beavers," said Bernice. "After that, you'll cross into grizzly territory. Then you're home. Well, if you're a dogg you're home—katts still have to cross the river. Over here, though, it's beaver, grizzlies, dogg. In that order."

Grizzly bears? thought Oscar. He just hoped they weren't hangry, too.

Chapter 44

As the two blue jays flew away, a new bird appeared.

A whirlybird. The WBN traffic helicopter. Francine the ferret was hanging out of the open side door.

"Hello, Violet and Romaldo!" the ferret shouted through a bullhorn as the chopper hovered about fifty feet above the cliff. "How'd you two like to win big money on the Weasel Broadcasting Network's top-rated quiz show?"

"Will there be snacks?" Violet shouted up to the helicopter.

"Oodles, honey. We're live tomorrow, eleven a.m. eastern, ten central, at the Wilderness Reserve welcome center."

"You mean that smelly shack near the gate?" yelled Romaldo.

"Exactly!" the ferret shouted back. "We're fixing the place up a little. There will be a glam tent, Violet. With gowns, makeup professionals, and fur stylists!"

"Yummy!" purred Violet, jumping up and down for joy.

"Be there. Profess your love. And you'll win an all-expenses-paid vacation to a romantic tropical island."

"Awesome!" shouted Romaldo. "More crashing waves."

"Can you fly us back to our camps?" asked Violet.

"Oh, you're not spending another night in that cramped RV, Violet. We're setting up a deluxe spa tent for you at the welcome center."

"Do I get a tent, too?" asked Romaldo. "I need a new puffy-sleeved shirt."

"You've got it," said the ferret. "So make your way to the welcome center. Quickly. We'll meet you there. Everything will be taken care of!"

"You sure you can't give us a ride?" shouted Molly.

"Sorry, dear, no. This wind is too nasty for a helicopter landing. But, here." The ferret tossed down four medallions attached to lanyards. "Bob the bear gave me those. They're badges that will grant you permission to safely cross through any zone on your way home."

"Cool," said Oscar, scooping one off the ground and hanging the lanyard around his neck. "It's like a VIP all-access pass!"

The wind gusted. The helicopter rocked.

"We have to leave!" shouted the ferret. "Safe travels. See you at the gatehouse. Oh, and don't tell your families."

"We can't!" shouted Molly, with a look to Violet and Romaldo. "We don't have phones!"

"Perfect. Let's keep this a big surprise...for everybody!"

Because the ferret knew (even though she wasn't saying it) that the biggest surprise would not be Phineas Fatt wooing Violet Hissleton in front of millions on *Furry Family Feud*.

It would be Romaldo Montahugh doing the wooing and Phineas doing the weeping.

And that would kick off TV's furriest, nastiest, most action-packed family feud ever!

Chapter 45

Oscar watched as the WBN helicopter battled the swirling winds and, finally, flew away.

That's when the torrential rain started up again.

"Okay, everybody," he said, trying to sound like his Dogg Scout pack leader. "We have to hike it out of here."

"On our feet?" whined Romaldo. "I've already done soooo much walking."

"Can't we call a cab?" said Violet. "Maybe hire a horse?"

Molly rolled her eyes. "No, Violet. We're in the wilderness. There are no taxicabs. The only horses are way over in the equestrian section and they're all here on vacation."

"Well, that's not fair," huffed Violet.

"I agree," said Romaldo. He took both of Violet's paws. "But you, my dear, are fairer than fair. The fairest maid in all the land."

Violet broke the handhold. "Maid? Do you expect me to clean up after you? Because doggs are nowhere as clean as katts."

"True, perhaps," said Romaldo. "But we're not the ones tracking litter all over the house."

"You chase your own tail!" screamed Violet.

"You hock up hair balls!" Romaldo shouted back.

Now Oscar rolled his eyes. The two lovebirds weren't sounding so lovey-dovey anymore. In fact, they sounded grouchy, grumpy, and snippy. Hunger, gale-force winds, and torrential downpours can do that to you.

"We're hiking!" Oscar screamed to break up

the bickering. "Here. Everybody, put on a medallion." He handed out the lanyards. "They grant us permission to trespass in other creatures' zones."

"Which means," said Molly, "we may not get pelted with acorns or stunkified by skunks."

"I'm still hungry," pouted Violet.

"As am I," proclaimed Romaldo.

"Can't you just say, 'me, too'?" asked Violet,

with an exasperated exhale. "Does everything have to be poetical with you?"

"The poet's eye, in a fine frenzy rolling—"

Violet stomped both feet, which splashed mud all over her fur. "Knock. It. Off." She whirled around to face Oscar. "Lead on, little dogg. Let's hike. And Molly? I'm hiking with you. If I'm going to be a TV star tomorrow, I need some tips..."

Chapter 46

Molly hung back with Violet as Oscar and Romaldo led the march into the woods and past the bright-yellow warning signs: BEAVERS ONLY BEYOND THIS POINT. TRESPASSERS WILL BE GNAWED AND NIBBLED.

"So," said Molly, "you're going to be on TV with Romaldo?"

Violet sighed. "I guess. He's always saying 'the course of true love never did run smooth' but I didn't expect it to be this bumpy."

"Well, you have options."

"I know. I have all sorts of wardrobe decisions to make…"

"You can also choose who you do the show with."

"Huh?"

Molly took a deep breath. Part of her hated herself for what she was about to say. Part of her knew she had to say it to protect her own dreams and ambitions.

"You could declare your love for Phineas Fatt instead of Romaldo!"

"Wha-hut?"

"Think about it!"

"If you were to, oh, I don't know, one day marry Phineas Fatt," Molly gushed, "it would make Grandmama Theodosia so happy! Plus, you'd never have to worry about Romaldo's head being so lost in the clouds that he forgets to take care of you down here on the ground. Why, if you married Phineas..."

"Ewww..."

"Your picnic basket would always be full! You'd have limousines to whisk you wherever you wanted to go. You'd have fourteen different umbrellas and raincoats and galoshes, whenever it rained."

"True," said Violet. "Phineas *is* filthy rich."

Molly nodded eagerly. "Richest katt in Kattsburgh. He probably has enough money to, I don't know, send your favorite cousin to the finest acting school in all the land."

"So," said Violet, "is that why you're acting as if me marrying Phineas Fatt is such a great idea?"

Hearing it said so bluntly (and honestly), Molly was totally ashamed of herself. "Kind of, sort of."

"No, thanks, Molly," said Violet. "I think I'll

stick with Romaldo. Yes, he is a poetic fool. But that's not his whole story. First impressions can often be misleading." Violet scampered faster. "Romaldo? Darling? Wait for me!"

Romaldo spun around and threw open his arms. "I would wait a thousand years for one moment in your paws!"

"Oh, that's bee-yoo-tee-full," said a beaver chomping on a chewy chunk of bark. "Just bee-yoo-tee-full. But you two are doggs. And you two are katts. This, in case you can't read, is the beaver zone! Prepare to have your ankles nibbled!"

Chapter 47

Oscar held out his arms protectively as a dozen angry beavers came waddling out of the bushes flapping their canoe-paddle tails.

Molly, Romaldo, and Violet stood behind him as the eager beavers emerged.

"Geezo, Pete," said one, looking up at the downpour. "So much rain in one day. It's like swimming in a river on dry land."

"Settle down, Bucky," said the beaver who seemed to be in charge. "We have some uninvited guests. We need to figure out what to do about 'em."

"Yeah," said another. "These four are giving us a lot to *chew* over."

All the beavers snorted back laughs. There was a chorus of happy chortles. "Oh, good one. Clever, clever. Touché!"

"Speaking of chewing," joked another, "forget potato chips. Wood Chips are my favorite snack."

There was more snorting and jolly chuckling.

Oscar stepped forward. "We all have these!" he boldly declared, showing everybody his safe passage medallion.

"Oooh," said the head beaver, admiring Oscar's medal. "Niiiice. Excellent craftsmanship. Check out the carving, you guys. That took some nifty toothwork."

"Wouldn't want to be that carver's orthodontist," said the beaver named Bucky.

"Bob the bear gave them to us," said Molly.

"Oooh," said all the beavers. "Bob. The. Bear. Impressive. They know Bob. The bear."

"We only wish to pass through your humble territory on our way home to the dogg and katt zones," declared Romaldo.

"Oooh," said Bucky. "He talks pretty. Smooth as birch bark."

"Romaldo and I are going to declare our love on national TV," said Violet, reaching out to, once again, take Romaldo's paw.

"Sweet," said the head beaver. "We love love. I propose we all raise a twig to your joyous, if strange, union. I mean, in case you haven't noticed, he's a dogg and you're a katt. That would be like me declaring my love for a wolf or a coyote. But here."

He yanked a root out of the soggy ground and tried to hand it to Violet and Romaldo.

"We munch to your happiness. It's sarsaparilla. Tastes just like root beer. Because, hello, it's a root!"

"Um, no, thank you," said Violet.

"I'll pass," added Romaldo, smacking his lips to clean away the bad taste of imagining he'd just eaten dirt.

"They're holding out for a maple stick," Bucky whispered behind his paw. "Can you blame them? A maple stick tastes like pancakes, only crunchier."

"Thank you so much for the, uh, celebration," said Oscar. "But we really need to keep heading south. We still have the grizzly bear zone to pass through."

"Ha!" laughed Bucky. "Good luck with that one. They might swat those lanyards right off your necks before they read 'em. With grizzlies, it's claw first and ask questions later."

"That's what my brother, Blaze, always says," muttered Molly.

"So your brother is a bear?"

"No. He's a katt."

"A bear cat? Like those ones across the river whose pee smells like popcorn?"

"No, he...oh, never mind. Oscar? The sun is starting to set. We need to hurry along."

"That we do," said Oscar. "Thank you for granting us safe passage through your territory."

"No problem," said the head beaver. "But be careful on your journey."

"Right," said Oscar. "The grizzlies."

"And the flood."

"Excuse me?"

The beaver flicked his flipper to the raging river just beyond the stumps of trees the bucktoothed rodents had recently chopped down.

"That water is rising fast," said the beaver.

"We know our rivers," added Bucky. "That one's going to jump its banks in under an hour."

"Um, don't you guys build dams?" said Molly. "In rivers? Don't dams stop floods?"

"Sure," said Bucky, picking a splinter out of his

teeth. "But we don't do any kind of construction work when we're on vacation."

"So," said the leader, "stick to the high ground. Otherwise, you might win another prize to go with your shiny new medallions: a free, one-way ticket to the whitewater rapids. And then a plunge over that eighty-foot-tall waterfall downstream. The one that dumps straight into the ocean!"

Chapter 48

The sun set and the forest was plunged into darkness as Molly and the others made their way through the beaver zone.

Molly could hear the surging river just beyond the trees and underbrush to her right. She could also hear the beaver's warnings ringing in her ears: "It's going to jump its banks!"

A flood was coming. This was not a great time to be outdoors.

"Okay," said Oscar, gesturing to a new set of

yellow warning signs. "Here we go. The grizzly bear zone."

"Remember to show them your all-access pass!" said Molly.

"Use the flashlight in your phones to illuminate them!" suggested Romaldo.

Molly turned around. Slowly.

"We don't have phones," she seethed. "Remember?"

Violet gave another cute shoulder shrug. "Oopsie."

"The storm is ending," said Oscar. "The moon is coming out. That should give us enough light to show our medallions."

Molly nodded. "We'll be okay. Bob promised us safe passage, and he's a bear."

"So these grizzlies are his cousins," remarked Romaldo. "Much as Oscar is mine."

"Only they're faster," said Oscar.

"Huh?" wondered Violet.

"I can run twenty-seven miles per hour," said Oscar.

"He's the fastest runner on his tennis ball

team," said Molly, remembering that tidbit of Oscar trivia (because Oscar mentioned it all the time).

"That's right," said Oscar proudly. "But even I can't outrun a grizzly. Not on any terrain, uphill or down. They may weigh more than seven hundred pounds, but they can clip along at *thirty-five* miles per hour."

"Hang on," said Romaldo. "I'm attempting to do the math. Five minus seven, bring over a one…"

"They're faster than us!" screamed Molly. "Okay? So if you see a bear, don't run. Just show them your medallion."

And, of course, that's when a giant grizzly bear stepped out of the shadows between two massive oak trees.

"Where do you four think you're going?" growled the bear.

"Um, hi," said Molly, flashing the bear her best toothpaste commercial smile. "I'm Molly Hissleton and these are my traveling companions. We all have badges."

"So?" whined the bear.

257

"So your cousin Bob gave them to us."

"Bob? The superintendent? Has a big belly he likes to scratch at inappropriate times?"

"That's right. He said these medallions would grant us safe passage through any zone in the Eastern Wilderness Reserve."

The grizzly bear stretched open its mouth wide and roared.

The air stank of smoked salmon.

Now two more grizzlies moseyed into the clearing.

"What's wrong, Gus?" asked one.

"Nothing, Muh-ther."

"Then why are you roaring?"

"And why do you have to keep nagging me with so many questions all the time?"

"Gus?"

"Yes, Muh-ther?"

"Go back to your den. Hibernate."

"But it's not winter."

"So?" said the other, gruffer grizzly. "Get a head start."

"Yes, Father," said Gus. Then he lumbered off.

The father bear stepped forward. The forest floor shook and quaked as he did. "Sorry about Gus. He's a teenager."

Molly and Oscar exchanged a glance. They understood. So were Romaldo and Violet.

"So," boomed the poppa bear, "which of you are the dogg and katt lovebirds?"

Molly and Oscar immediately pointed to Romaldo and Violet. "Them!"

Romaldo did one of his arm-swooping, hand-swirling bows. Violet curtsied.

"You're the ones Bob told us about?" asked the momma grizzly. "The ones who are going to be on TV tomorrow?"

"Yes, ma'am," said Romaldo. "We're going to be a surprise!"

"Eleven o'clock eastern," added Violet, striking a glamorous pose. "Ten central."

"That's why we need to deliver them to the gatehouse tonight," said Molly, making her smile even brighter.

"We have to choose our wardrobe," said Romaldo.

"Have our fur and makeup done," added Violet.

Molly was smiling so widely her cheeks hurt. "So if you folks don't mind…"

"Eh-heh-heh-heh," chuckled the poppa grizzly. "This is gonna be good. Bob told us all about it."

"He sure did," laughed the momma bear. "Can't wait to see it. He and Francine, the TV ferret, have cooked up something superspecial this time. We'll be watching, for sure. Eleven o'clock eastern. Ten central."

"Live on the Weasel Broadcasting Network," added her husband.

"You guys, like, have a TV?" asked Violet. "Here in the wilderness?"

The two bears nodded.

"Battery powered," said the father.

"Wouldn't go camping without it," added the mother. "Well, we don't want to hold you folks up. Can't have a TV show without the stars. Just flash those badges to any other grizzlies you bump into on your way and—"

Suddenly, from off in the distance, came a frantic cry for help.

"Help! We're being swept away here! We don't do so good with water."

Molly and Oscar bolted for the riverbank. The swift-moving bears were there in a flash, too. Romaldo and Violet brought up the rear.

The river's angry swells and choppy rapids glistened in the moonlight.

"There!" said Oscar, pointing south.

About fifty yards upstream, he could see several katt heads bobbing up and down in the middle of the raging river.

"Those are the alley katts we met earlier!" said Molly.

"Help!" shouted Knuckles, the gang leader. "Save us! We don't want to drown."

Molly turned to Oscar. "They probably don't want to take a ride over that waterfall we heard about, either!"

Oscar got a determined look on his face. "We have to rescue them!"

"But they're katts," said the father bear. "And you're a dogg."

"I don't care," said Oscar. "Because right now, they're also in trouble!"

Chapter 49

The two giant bears splashed into the raging rapids and made their way to the center of the stream.

"Time to do some katt-fishing!" they roared.

"We need to form a chain!" shouted Romaldo, sounding completely focused, which completely surprised Oscar.

"Molly?" cried Violet. "You're the shortest. You take the position closest to the shore."

"Oscar?" said Romaldo, fighting the current

and wading into deeper water. "You plant your-self about three feet away from Molly."

"I'll be three feet from you," Violet told Oscar. She was sloshing through the rapids, too.

"And I'll be the one closest to the bears," shouted Romaldo. "Bears?"

"Yeah?"

"When you pluck a katt out of the stream, kindly pass them along to me, and I'll pass them along to Violet, who will pass them on to Oscar, who will hand them off to Molly, who will safely place them on the shore."

"Sounds like a plan," said the two grizzlies.

"Romaldo's very good at planning things," said Violet proudly.

"Really?" said Oscar, sounding surprised, maybe even stunned. "He is?"

"Those secret codes he's always doing?" said Violet. "Our whole rendezvous on the Giant Stones? That kind of stuff takes planning, kiddo!"

The alley katts floated closer.

"Here they come!" said the mother bear.

"I see 'em!" said the poppa bear.

"Steady," proclaimed Romaldo, very heroically. "Steady!"

"Help!" screamed Knuckles, the first in the ragged line of alley katts being swept downstream. "Save us, grizzly bears! And then, uh, please don't eat us!"

"Got him!" shouted the mother grizzly, plucking Knuckles out of the flood-swollen water by the scruff of his neck. She used her mouth—careful to use a soft clamp technique instead of a bite—and then dropped the relieved katt into her paws. "Just like grabbing salmon out of a barrel!"

"Toss him to me, oh, noble grizzly!" shouted Romaldo.

The bear did.

The bears scooped all the alley katts out of the whitewater rapids and passed them off to the katts and doggs.

"Wow!" Oscar shouted to Romaldo and Violet.

"You two are way smarter than I realized!"

"Never judge a book by its cover!" said Violet.

"Unless I'm on it," joked Molly. "Then you know it has to be good!"

They all laughed. It was the kind of laughter that feels good right after you've all gone through something dangerous and extremely exciting together.

"Hey!" commanded a stern voice. "Stop that!"

"Who's yelling at us now?" wondered the biggest grizzly.

"Me!"

Everybody looked up.

"It's that pesky bald eagle!" said Molly. "They're only supposed to hunt during the day!"

"Oh, I'm not hunting," thundered the eagle, circling over the river. "But I have my eagle eye on all of you. Interspecies mingling and cooperation? That is against all the rules of this wilderness. It is against the rules of civilized society, as well. No intermingling! No cooperating! Definitely no rescuing of your enemies! You should all be ashamed of yourselves. You are a blight on the natural order of the animal kingdom."

"And you," said Violet, "are in the wrong zone, beak boy. Head back to bird land. Unless you want to see what my cuz Molly and I can do with the help of twelve very grateful, and probably hungry, alley katts."

"Yeah!" shouted Knuckles from the safety of the shore. "These folks saved our lives. We owe them. Anything they want? We'll do it for 'em. Even if it means tearing out a few of your tail feathers the next time you swoop down low enough for us to claw your butt."

The eagle harrumphed grumpily. "You hooligans haven't heard the last of me!"

"Yes, we have," said the mother bear, covering her ears with her paws. "In fact, I can't hear a thing!"

And as the eagle soared away, the six rescuers laughed together even louder.

Chapter 50

Molly was impressed by her cousin Violet, who was making sure none of the rescued alley katts were seriously injured.

"If any of you are in pain," said Violet, "chew on a little of this willow bark. It's nature's aspirin."

Now Molly's jaw was hanging open. Violet seemed to know the same kind of stuff about natural remedies that Molly's mom did! And Molly's mom was a nurse.

Violet must've seen the surprised look on Molly's face. "I'm going to be a doctor," she told Molly.

Molly did a double take. "Seriously?"

"Oh, did you think I was a ditzy airhead?"

"Kind of, sort of."

"Okay. Fur sure I like a little pampering. Nice fur and nails. But, Molly? No one is just one thing. Of course, I'll admit, I've been a little dopey lately."

"A little?"

Violet sighed dreamily. "Love will do that to you, kiddo. But did you know that Romaldo's not just a poet? He wants to be an architect. And did you know the very famous dogg architect Frank Lloyd Bite said that every great architect is, necessarily, a great poet?"

"Um, no. I don't memorize many famous architect quotes. Mostly movie scripts and TV dramas."

"Well, Romaldo has big dreams and wants to design big projects. Like bridges and buildings and—"

"Dams!" said Molly. "That's what we need. Upstream. Oscar? Romaldo? I have an idea!"

Molly quickly presented her plan. It was actually very ingenious.

"That eagle's not going to like it," said Oscar.

"Who cares?" said Romaldo. "We must dare to be bold! I think it's an excellent plan, Molly. Now we must execute it, posthaste, as the river continues to rise."

"So where's the best place for a dam?" wondered Oscar.

"Stand back," said Molly. "I'm about to launch one of my species-mingling, total cooperation plans!"

Molly cupped her paws over her mouth and screeched an earsplitting "Eee-eee-eee!"

She waited.

Then she screeched again. "Eee-eee-eee!"

"All right, already," said Bernie, landing on a nearby tree.

"We heard you the first time," said Bernice, landing beside him.

"We need your help," Molly told the two blue jays. "We need to locate the source of the flooding."

"Um, it's the river," said Bernie.

"Can we go back to sleep now?" asked Bernice, stifling a yawn with the tip of her wing.

"We know it's the river that's flooding," said Oscar, knocking some water out of his ear. "We were just in it."

"But where, pray tell, is the best place to dam it up?" asked Romaldo.

Violet sighed. "See, Molly? He's poetical and practical. A very civil civil engineer."

"Oh, I get it," said Bernie. "You want us to fly up the river and scout it out?"

"Actually," said Molly, "we want you to fly to the giraffe zone and ask them to scout it out."

"They should be willing to help," said Violet. "Because a flood doesn't discriminate."

"It could wipe away everything and everybody in its path," added Romaldo.

"And," said Oscar, "giraffes have excellent eyesight. Why, they can spot a lion from a whole kilometer away!"

"And," Oscar went on, "their long necks put those eyes in an excellent position to quickly survey the whole river."

The two blue jays were staring at Oscar in amazement.

"How come you know so much about giraffes, kid?" asked Bernie.

"I have a Dogg Scout wildlife trivia merit badge."

"Hurry," said Molly. "We have to move quickly."

"You got it!" said Bernie. He and Bernice took off.

"Come on, Oscar," said Molly. "We need to go back and chat with some beavers!"

Chapter 51

Oscar led the way back through the woods to the beaver zone.

The beavers were all gathered around a campfire that wasn't lit so everybody could snack on the kindling.

"We need you guys to build a dam!" Oscar told the head beaver, whose name, he learned, was Bruno. "Otherwise, creatures in zones up and down both sides of this river are going to get swept away."

"And," added Molly, "tumble over that waterfall you told us about."

Bruno rubbed his furry face and thought about it. "We are on vacation. Dam building is our job. You're not supposed to do your job when you're on vacation. You're supposed to have family fun..."

"Your whole family can join in!" said Molly.

"And have fun," added Oscar. "We're lining up some rhinoceroses to do the bulldozing."

"Seriously?" said Bruno. "Rhinos? Awesome."

"We'll also have a crew of squirrels to bend the tree branches to make them easier to saw and gnaw," said Oscar. "And the grizzly bears will scoop rocks and junk out of the river for you guys."

"And," said Molly, "the binturongs will be there. Making the whole area smell like a carnival with their popcorn pee!"

"Woo-hoo!" said Bruno, leaping for joy. "Bucky? Hacksaw? Chisel Tooth? Grab your families. We're heading upriver to build a dam for fun! There's going to be popcorn! Well, the smell of popcorn..."

"Um, what about the skunks?" Oscar whispered to Molly. "What can they do?"

Molly thought about it, then snapped her claws. "Security guards. There might be certain creatures who don't like the idea of all of us working together..."

Oscar nodded glumly. "Yeah. Like your grandmother and my grandfather."

Molly nodded. "The skunks can keep them away from our construction site."

"By the way—did you know your cousin Violet was so smart?"

"Nope. But she's going to be a doctor. And what about your cousin Romaldo? The wannabe architect?"

Oscar shrugged. "Never had a clue. Guess it pays to get to know somebody before you go ahead and figure out who you think they are."

"Yeah."

"Hey! You two! TWEET!"

Oscar and Molly looked up. Bernie and Bernice were back.

"The giraffes found the perfect spot," said

Bernie. "And it wasn't on their hides. See what I did there? Because giraffes have spots on their—"

"We get it, Bernie," said Bernice. "We get it. Anyway, the ideal dam location is just upstream from the rhino zone."

"Bring your construction crew!" said Bernice. "We've got work to do!"

"Oh, so now you're a poet?" said Bernie.

"Nah, poetry is Romaldo's thing. I just rhyme some of the time."

"Let's go, everybody!" Molly called to the beavers.

And all through the night, with the skunks standing guard while the binturongs did their aromatherapy thing and the rhinos bulldozed up the mud and the grizzly bears scooped up rocks from the riverbed and the squirrels bent branches and the beavers gnawed and sawed, and the alley katts peeled and stripped bark with their claws, all the creatures, who had nothing in common, worked together to build the dam that would save them all.

Chapter 52

Molly woke up to the gentle sound of water trickling over the top of the dam.

She also had a twig in her mouth, because, after they finished building the dam, all the creatures had a big party (the rhinos had twinkle toes and could really dance). Exhausted at the end of the celebration, everybody just dropped to the ground and fell asleep. Unfortunately, Molly landed in a twig pile.

"Good morning, Molly!" said Oscar eagerly. He

had crumpled leaves and pine needles in his fur. "A lot of folks have already headed back to their own zones. It's just us, Violet and Romaldo, a couple squirrels, Knuckles the alley katt, a skunk or two, and Bucky the beaver."

"They put me in charge of dam maintenance!" said Bucky proudly.

"You all did a splendid job," said Romaldo, strolling over with Violet. They were holding paws.

"Liked your idea about the mud and pebbles in the substructure," Bucky told Romaldo. "You sure you're not part beaver?"

Romaldo smiled. "No. I just like to engineer clever solutions."

"And tricky secret codes!" added Violet.

"Thanks again for saving us," said Knuckles the alley katt, stretching and yawning in a sunny spot on the riverbank.

"Where's the rest of your crew?" asked Oscar.

"They went down to the grizzly zone for a fish fry. Me? I saw enough fish in that flood to last me a lifetime."

"Whoa," rumbled a voice coming up the trail. "Romaldo? Violet? What are you two doing here?"

It was Bob the bear. He wasn't alone. A snow-white polar bear wearing rose-colored granny glasses and grinning like crazy was ambling along behind him. She had white dreadlocks and a neck-lace of woven flowers draped around her neck.

"Far out!" said the polar bear. "Isn't this groovy? Katts and doggs and squirrels and beavers and skunks, all just hangin' out together, chillin'. You see what I'm talking about, Bob?"

"Yes, Momsy. I see it."

"This is what the world needs, man. Love, sweet love."

"Momsy?" said Molly, squinting as she moved forward.

"Hey, there. You have a twig in your mouth."

Molly spat it out. "Sorry. We've met before. I'm Molly Hissleton."

"And I'm Oscar Montahugh," said Oscar. "You helped us when we were lost on top of that snow-capped mountain, trying to find our way back to the Great Western Frontier Park."

"Solid," said Momsy, giggling. "I'm flashing back to that groovy scene. You two were cuddling and snuggling in the snow..."

"BECAUSE WE WERE COLD!" Molly and Oscar shouted together.

Momsy winked. "Sure. I can dig it...if that's the line you two lovebirds are laying down."

"We're. Not. Lovebirds!" said Molly.

"Actually, we're not birds at all," said Oscar.

Momsy winked again. "Cool. Like I said, I can dig it, man."

Bob whirled around to face Romaldo and Violet. "Thank goodness a certain little birdy told me where to find you two. You're supposed to be at my gatehouse. In your glam tents. Picking out your wardrobe. Getting your fur fluffed. Francine the ferret is counting on you both to, uh, make her show special."

"Sorry, sir," said Romaldo. "We humbly beg your forgiveness. Duty called. To be honest, in the face of a natural disaster threatening so many lives, we forgot all about our scheduled TV appearance."

"We had to build a dam to stop the flood," said Violet. "Otherwise, all sorts of creatures would've been washed out to sea."

"So you all worked together?" said Momsy. "You cooperated?"

"Oh, yeah," said Oscar. "We had giraffes, rhinos, alley katts—even a couple coyotes dropped by to lend a paw. They have excellent night vision, even without goggles."

Now Momsy turned to Bob. "I win, Robert. Creatures *can* get along if they try. It's like I always say, we're stronger together."

Bob slumped his shoulders. "Fine. Now, can we all go to my gatehouse and watch the live, special edition of *Furry Family Feud*?" He held up his paws to frame an imaginary billboard. "The Hissletons versus the Montahughs."

"I'm a Hissleton!" said Molly, beaming. "I'm also an excellent actress. I want to be on TV."

"I'll tell the ferret to make sure you're on the team," said Bob. "Let's go. Romaldo and Violet? We need you, too."

"What about Oscar?" demanded Molly.

Bob shrugged again. "Sure. Fine. Whatever. Come on. We don't want to keep your fans waiting."

"Not so fast, Bob," said Momsy, sounding a lot less flaky.

"But—"

"But nothing, man. You lost our little wager."

"But, Francine—"

"Can wait a few minutes more. I need to tell these four young'uns a little story before they truck on over to the ferret's game show."

Bob scratched his belly. "Okay. Fine. But don't take too long. The show is live at eleven and it's already eight thirty."

"Come on, children," said Momsy. "Walk with me. I want to tell you a tale about the Giant Stones."

"Oh," said Molly. "The one about the giants who lived across the sea from each other and were either in love or they hated each other's guts?"

"We've already heard that one," said Oscar. "Bob told it to us."

Momsy chuckled. "This is a different story. And it's even bigger than those giants. Because, Molly and Violet, Oscar and Romaldo, this story is about you. Well, your families—the Hissletons and the Montahughs. And something that happened, back in the day. Back when Bob and I weren't the only foolish young creatures falling in love."

Chapter 53

Meanwhile, at the entrance to the Eastern Wilderness Reserve, the Hissletons and the Montahughs were standing on opposite sides of the *Furry Family Feud* game show set.

Elephant security guards formed a barricade separating the two feuding families. Francine the ferret sat astride one of the elephants in a shaded howdah chair. She had to yell through a megaphone to be heard over the hissing, howling, barking, and baying.

"All right, everybody," she hollered. "Settle down."

"Thank you, Hissletons," said the ferret when the angry bickering settled down to a dull roar. "Thank you, Montahughs. Thank you all for appearing on today's show. *Furry Family Feud— Wild in the Wilderness* will be one for the ages. We go live at eleven."

The elephants trumpeted. They were the game show's band as well as its security guards.

Francine the ferret glanced at her watch. "It's only nine now. Plenty of time for our guest stars to show up..."

"Guest stars?" shouted Oscar's father, Duke. "Who's that gonna be?"

"Why, uh, your son, Oscar, of course," said the ferret, dabbing some sweat off her upper lip.

"And for our team?" asked Molly's father, Boomer.

"Your darling daughter, Molly."

"Let's hope she arrives safely," said Boomer. "We haven't heard from her this morning."

"She was on a rescue mission," sniffed Molly's mother. "Searching for her cousin Violet."

"I think she got, like, swept away in that flash

flood last night," said her brother, Blade.

"Blade?" boomed Molly's father. "Honestly. Don't say things like that!"

Blade shrugged. "I heard that, like, a whole bunch of alley katts were swept downstream when the river went rogue and jumped its banks—and nobody's seen them since!"

"And ain't nobody lookin' for 'em, neither!" cracked Duke. "'Cuz, hello, you said they was katts!"

"You tell 'em, son!" said Oscar's grandpa Max.

"I just did, Diddy. Turn up your hearing aids."

"Don't you be tellin' me what to do, boy," snarled Max.

"Qui-et!" shouted the ferret. The elephants blared their noses again. "You Montahughs are supposed to be feuding with the Hissletons, not each other."

"Aw, I can do both," said Duke. "I'm what they call a multitasker."

"You mean a multi-licker," said Boomer snidely.

"Hey! I heard that, katt! We doggs have excellent ears!"

"You also have ugly faces."

"Perfect!" said the ferret from her perch. "That's exactly the nasty kind of back-and-forth we need. Conflict. That's why everybody watches TV. They like to see contestants yelling at each other."

"Oh, we'll give you that," growled Grandpa Max. "We hate the Hissletons. Have for years."

"Perhaps," hissed Theodosia. "But we Hissletons hate you Montahughs more, Max. And you know why!"

Duke turned to his father, Max. "Why, Diddy? Why do we hate these particular katts even more than regular katts? Do their butts stink worse? Are their hair balls soggier?"

Now Boomer turned to his mother, Theodosia. "You know, Mumsy, the foul-smelling fleabag has a point. Why are these Montahugh doggs more despicable than any others?"

"Never mind!" Max told Duke.

"None of your business!" Theodosia told Boomer.

And that's when the doggs and katts found something new to bark and yowl about: Phineas

Fatt rolled up in his stretch limousine. And then he rolled out the door.

Literally.

"I'm here to cheer on the Hissletons," he announced, when he waddled to his feet. "And to propose marriage to my beloved Violet!"

"Did you hear that, you mangy mutts!" Boomer declared triumphantly. "Phineas Fatt plans on marrying my niece Violet. Our family is going to be filthy rich."

"And," Theodosia sneered at Max on the other side of the elephant, "you will simply remain filthy!" Then she curled her paw and scratched the air at him. "Mee-yow."

Chapter 54

Oscar found a small clearing where everybody could sit on a stump, log, or rock.

"Thank you," said Momsy, the hippie polar bear, settling into position, crossing her legs yoga style. "This spot is perfect, man. Very chill."

Oscar, Molly, Romaldo, and Violet found their own seats.

Romaldo and Violet, of course, were holding paws.

"I want to tell you young bloods a story," said Momsy.

"About the Giant Stones," said Oscar, trying to be helpful. "You already told us that part."

"Right. Well, back in the day, I was a licensed wedding officiant. Still am, as a matter of fact. Anyhow, there was a young couple, very much in love, man. Couldn't find anybody hip enough to marry them. Why? Because he was a dogg and she was a katt."

"Why, that's just like us!" Romaldo said to Violet. "I'm a dogg, and you're a katt."

Oscar and Molly exchanged an eye roll. *Well, duh,* they both wanted to say.

"As a last resort," Momsy continued, "since no katt or dogg preacher would help them out, the two lovebirds asked me to preside over their ceremony. I said, sure, because I'm all about love, sweet love. They were going to elope. To run off and get married secretly. No family. No friends. Just me and one witness—my boyfriend, Bob."

"The bear?" said Oscar. "The park super-intendent?"

"Well, back then he was just a pizza delivery bear into heavy metal, but he was my main man. Bob said yes and, on the big day, we all met on the Giant Stones at sunset."

"How very romantic," said Romaldo with a sigh. "The architectural silhouette of that natural staircase is so inspiring."

"Sounds like a perfect way to get married," said Violet. "Especially if you're busy going to med school."

"Yes, it was all pretty sweet," said Momsy. "Bob sang their favorite song."

"What was it?" asked Molly.

"'I Love My Dogg' by Katt Sneezins."

"Oh, that's a good one." Molly started humming a snatch of it.

"So, uh, not to be rude," said Oscar, "but what does this have to do with us?"

"Well," said Momsy, "a big rainstorm swept in off the ocean. It was a real fur soaker, man. All of a sudden, the katt and dogg were drenched. They started getting hangry. You know—hungry and angry."

Violet gave Romaldo a sheepish look and mouthed, *I'm sorry about yesterday.*

"As am I," said Romaldo.

"Soaked, missing their families, without any friends to remind them who they truly were, they started snarling and hissing at each other, big time," said Momsy. "They had a HUGE fight. Both of them said things I know they probably regretted saying later. How they'd been foolish to fall in love. How katts and doggs could never get along—just like katts and mice or doggs and squirrels. They were, they realized, natural enemies. And natural enemies could never become friends, let alone husband and wife. And so they flung their wedding rings into the crashing waves. It was a bad scene, man. Totally bummed me out. Bummed Bob out, too. Made Bob bitter. We broke up that day, too."

"Did the dogg and katt ever kiss and make up?" asked Violet.

Momsy shook her head sadly.

"Nope. They were too mad. Then they stayed mad. So mad, a family feud erupted—one that's been going on for years."

"You mean like the feud between the Montahughs and Hissletons?" said Oscar.

Momsy nodded solemnly. "Exactly like that. Because that dogg and katt whose love ended up on the rocks that fateful day? That was Max Montahugh and Theodosia Hissleton."

"Wait a second," said Molly. "Our grandparents?"

"They were in love?" said Oscar.

"Just like us?" said Violet.

Momsy nodded. "Can you dig it? They chose hate over love. And it's ruled their lives."

Chapter 55

Wait a second," said Molly. "Last night we proved that all those myths about sworn enemies for life are wrong. They're just hate-filled stories we've told ourselves too many times."

Oscar nodded. "Different kinds of creatures *can* get along. They can help one another in an emergency. Those squirrels and beavers and bears sure did."

"Which means," said Momsy, "they can do it whenever they choose to do it."

"They can fall in love, too," said Romaldo and Violet.

"And they can make their cousins hurl if they keep making goo-goo eyes at each other," said Molly. "But, okay. Love is better than hate."

"Easier, too," said Momsy. "Takes a whole lot of work to stay angry as long as your grandparents have, man. Leads to sour stomachs and pinched faces, too."

Oscar turned to Romaldo and Violet. "And we were wrong about you two. You're not just a flaky poet, Romaldo."

"Um, thanks," said Romaldo. "I think."

"And you're not just a dopey space cadet," Molly told Violet. "You've got brains to go with your beauty."

"Oh-kay," said Violet.

Molly rubbed her paws together. "So now, we want to help you two make your dreams come true."

"Yes!" said Oscar. "We do. Uh, how are we gonna do that, Molly?"

"Well, I have an idea for a little scene that might lead to a happily ever after for Romaldo and Violet."

"Of course you do!" said Oscar. "Because you're a brilliant actress and you know how to make a scene sing!"

Molly bowed slightly. "And you, Oscar, are an intrepid Dogg Scout. Not to mention the fastest runner on your tennis ball team."

"True. True."

"So what's the plan, children?" asked Momsy.

Molly beamed. The others were hanging on her every word. She was in the spotlight and she was loving it. "I think we can create a tragic tale that will make our grandparents fall in love with the idea of Romaldo and Violet being in love."

"Is such a thing possible?" wondered Romaldo.

"Hey, when squirrels help doggs and grizzly bears rescue alley katts, anything is possible."

"I can dig it, sister!" shouted Momsy. "Lay it on me."

Molly was about to explain her idea when she heard an annoying peeping overhead.

The obnoxious eagle was back.

"I see you down there!" the eagle declared. "Doggs and katts and a bear. All together in a zone that's not your own."

"Well you're not in the bird zone, either!" Oscar shouted up at the sky.

"The sky is my domain!" boomed the eagle. "I rule it, mightily!"

Once again, Molly cupped her hands over her snout and sent up a shrill "Eee-eee-eee!"

"We're on it!" said Bernie, swooping in from out of nowhere.

"You rule the sky?" Bernice shouted at the eagle. "Not for long, you follicl-y challenged cue ball. It's time for mob rule, baldy!"

Two dozen blue jays zoomed in from wherever they'd been, formed a tight squadron, and chased the eagle away.

"Far out," said Momsy. "Even the blue jays want to help you two lovebirds."

"So what's the plan, Molly?" asked Violet.

"We long to hear you speak of it!" added Romaldo.

"We're gonna need a few more players," said Molly, her mental wheels spinning. "Bucky the beaver. Knuckles the alley katt. Bernie and Bernice. We're in the scene, too, Oscar."

"What're we gonna do?"

"Make both our families remember how they felt when you and I were lost in the wilderness and they all thought we were never coming home!"

Chapter 56

Francine the ferret was fretting.

It was ten thirty. *Furry Family Feud* was supposed be on the air, LIVE, in thirty minutes.

Phineas Fatt had arrived (and eaten all the food in the VIP tent) but there was still no sign of the real stars: Romaldo and Violet. When those two showed up and declared their love for each other in front of their warring families, the fur was really going to fly.

"Where the heck is Oscar?" grumbled Duke. "We might need him in case this quiz show has questions about stuff the rest of us don't know."

"Oh," said Boomer Hissleton snidely, "you mean every question in every category except the ones about peeing on shrubbery?"

"Hey, you folks ain't got Molly, neither!" taunted Duke. "So the only questions you're gonna be able to answer are the ones about licking yourselves in awkward positions!"

Francine realized that the two fathers were hurling insults because neither Theodosia nor Max was currently on the set.

"Where are the two old geezers?" she whispered into her headset.

"They're on their way back," came word from the control room. "Looks like they both wandered off to a nearby meadow."

"Together?"

"No. Separately. But you know old folks. They like to wander. And use the bathroom."

"What did I miss?" growled Grandpa Max when he returned to the set.

"Aw, we're just hurling some insults at them Hissletons, Diddy."

"And did you return fire, Boomer?" asked Grandma Hissleton when she took her place with the rest of her assembled family.

"Indeed I did, Mumsy," said Boomer.

"It's, like, so easy to make fun of doggs," added Blade. "Like the one who went to the flea circus and stole the whole show!"

Just then, Knuckles, soaking wet and looking bedraggled, came stumbling out of the woods, spitting out murky river water.

"Oh, dear!" cried Molly's mother, Fluffy. "It's one of the missing alley katts!"

"We heard you guys were, like, all dead," said Blade. "Washed away in the flash flood."

"I am the sole survivor," said Knuckles, very dramatically. "Only I lived to tell the tale!"

"What happened?" gasped the ferret, eager for the scoop. (She did news for the WBN as well as game shows.)

"It's like the kid over there said." Knuckles flapped a weak paw in Blade's direction. "A dozen of us were out playing in the meadow near the river when, all of a sudden, down pours a torrential downpour. We're soaked. Our fur clinging to our skin."

"Ew, gross," said Fifi.

"The river rose!" Knuckles continued. "Fast and angry. It jumped its banks and swept us away. We were whisked downstream. I was lucky enough to grab hold of a tree branch as I raced through the rapids just before the big waterfall could dump me in the ocean. My friends and family weren't so fortunate. They were all washed out to sea!"

"It's true!" said a bucktoothed beaver scurrying into the clearing. "We tried to dam up the river but it was too strong and swift for us. We couldn't chop down trees fast enough to hold it back."

Now two blue jays flitted into view and landed near the game show's scoreboard.

"The alley katts weren't the only ones washed away!" said the male.

"We saw giraffes, hippos, squirrels, and skunks floating downstream!" said the female.

"Any of my family?" asked the beaver, sounding choked up. Like he had a chunk of sawdust in his throat. "Any beavers?"

"Nope," said the male blue jay. "The beavers are excellent swimmers."

"Much better than katts or doggs," added the female.

"Oh, dear," said Boomer. "My daughter and niece were out in that storm last evening. They're katts!"

"Did you see any doggs being washed over that there waterfall?" asked Duke. "Maybe one in a puffy-sleeved shirt? Another who looks like this picture in my wallet here?"

And that's when Oscar and Molly made their (very) dramatic entrance.

The ferret kicked her camera operator. "Film this! We might be able to use it in the show!"

"We...survived...Dad," sputtered Oscar.

"Just barely," said Molly, her legs wobbly as she staggered and lurched forward.

Her mother and father ran over to catch her with open arms while Oscar teetered and tottered over to his terrified parents.

"What about your cousin Violet?" asked Molly's mother while Oscar's mother asked him much the same thing. "Where's Romaldo?"

Molly and Oscar looked at each other.

Molly started sobbing. Then she wailed and gnashed her teeth and threw her arm up to her forehead to fight off a swoon.

"We don't know!" she shrieked. "But...we... think..."

She bit her lip. She couldn't go on.

So Oscar finished for her.

"We think they were washed away in that flash flood with the alley katts and swept down to the waterfall where they tumbled over the edge and landed on the jagged rocks in the ocean!"

Chapter 57

*N*ot *a dry eye in the house!* thought Molly as she prepared to emote her way through her monologue. *Everybody's sobbing!*

"Oh, was there ever a tale filled with more woe than that of sweet Cousin Violet and a drowning dogg named Romaldo?"

"Heavens, no!" said Molly's father, his voice breaking. "Violet can't be dead. She was so full of life."

"Yeah, but then she, you know, drowned," said Blade (who could be kind of thick).

"Romaldo had all sorts of life and stuff in him, too," said Oscar's father, blubbering a little. "Sure, most of that stuff was phony poetry baloney, but, dang, Romaldo was family."

"If only we could have them both back with us right now!" said Oscar.

"What would you give for that to be true?" Molly asked dramatically.

"Why, I'd give anything for that!" said Oscar's dad, sniffling back a tear. "What am I gonna tell Romaldo's mother?"

"He was soooo cool," said Oscar's sister, Fifi. "The coolest."

"Why, I'd give Violet whatever she wanted if it meant having her back with us," said Molly's father, dabbing at his damp eyes.

"As would I!" said her mother.

"Whatever," said her brother.

Molly looked to her grandmother.

And didn't like what she saw.

Theodosia Hissleton's eyes were bone dry and narrowing into angry slits.

Something was wrong.

And Oscar was about to give Romaldo and Violet their cue.

"Oh, if only they were not lost in the flood," Oscar wailed, sounding a little stilted, because he didn't know how to memorize lines and make them sound like they weren't memorized lines. "Why, we'd all give them their fondest wish, no matter what it might be."

That's when, to the gasps of everybody (except Grandmama Theodosia and Oscar's grandpa Max), Violet and Romaldo strode into the clearing holding hands. Bob the bear was walking behind them.

"It's a miracle!" declared Bob the bear, who was probably the most overblown, scenery-chewing, hammy performer in the cast. "It's a miracle, I tell you. An unbelievable, incredible, one-of-a-kind, never-gonna-happen-again miracle. Look what I found! Down near the waterfall. Violet and Romaldo. I'm not sure how these two crazy knuckleheads did it but they saved each other! Right before they would've plummeted over the falls and crashed on the rocks and been eaten by sharks if there was anything left of them to eat!"

"Yes," declared Romaldo. "What Bob says is true."

"We saved each other's lives!" cried Violet.

"And in so doing," said Romaldo, gently kissing Violet's paw, "we fell in love!"

Another gasp from the crowd.

"You what?" snarled Oscar's father.

"Pardon moi?" said Molly's father. "I don't believe I heard that correctly."

"It's totally true," said Violet. "We're in love! Sure, he's a dogg and I'm a katt. But that doesn't matter."

"For love is blind," said Romaldo, striking a very poetic pose. "Love does not see what sort of fur or whiskers or feathers or leathery hide you have on the outside. Love only sees what's on the inside! Love looks first at your heart."

"Cut!" shouted the ferret. "Save it for the cameras, you two. We're not on the air for fifteen more minutes."

"You knew about this?" said Oscar's dad.

"Maybe," squeaked the ferret.

"Well, how is that possible?" said Molly's father. "They only fell in love last night. During the flood..."

"Um, I just know things," said the ferret. "I've got intuition. It's why I'm such a good reporter.

"But I want to marry Violet!" blubbered Phineas, who'd been sitting on the ground, scooping chunks of wet tuna out of a can with his paw.

"Do you love her?" demanded Romaldo.

"No, not really," said Phineas. "But I love wedding feasts! And wedding cake. Italian wedding soup is good, too..."

And that's when Molly's grandmother exploded.

"Enough!" She glared at Violet and then Molly. "Your foolish and juvenile charade cannot fool me, grandchildren!"

"Or me!" barked Oscar's grandpa Max. "Mark my words the way I'd mark a tree: you two ain't never ever gonna get married!"

Chapter 58

Oscar cringed when he saw how angry his grandpa Max was.

"You two weren't never in no danger!" Grandpa Max snapped.

"I believe you're using a triple negative, old bean," said Molly's father. "If they were 'not never' in 'no danger' that would mean that at some point they *were* in no danger, which, even on its own, makes no sense…"

"Aw, shuddup, Boomer!" declared Molly's grandmama Theodosia. "Your melodramatic daughter, Molly, tried to trick us with her cheap, amateurish theatrics. Tugging at our heartstrings with a sad tale of Violet plunging over a waterfall. Boo-hoo-hoo, indeed."

"Besides," snapped Grandpa Max, "we know that you, Theodosia, don't have any heartstrings to pluck because you ain't got no heart."

"And you, Maximillian, have no brain or sense of proper grammar."

"Don't make no never mind." Grandpa Max whirled around to glare at Romaldo. "We know the truth, boy. You and this Violet katt was down on the Giant Stones yesterday, holding hands and acting all lovey-dovey."

Grandma Theodosia turned on Violet. "We know all about it, you devious and ungrateful child. For a noble eagle recently told us what he witnessed from high above!"

There was an annoying squawk overhead. "I most certainly did!" shouted the circling eagle. His voice was even more pompous than usual. "Your grandparents and I had a little one-on-one time over in yon meadow. I told them both—separately, of course—what twisted and abnormal notions you two had been contemplating. I advised them of your pernicious plot! A katt in love with a dogg? Ridiculous. It goes against the natural order of things. It will not be allowed! No, sir. Not on my watch!"

The two blue jays, who were still perched on top of the game show scoreboard, turned to each other. They had scowls on their beaks.

"Bernice?"

"I'm right there with you, Bernard."

"It's mob time!"

"Eee-eee-eee!"

The two birds streaked into the sky like scrambled fighter jets. They were soon joined by three dozen other screeching jays. In tight formation, they executed a synchronized loop-the-loop and attacked the eagle. As they chased him away, a few eagle feathers drifted down. The big blowhard of a bird would end the day a little balder, mostly on his butt.

"Did you capture that aerial action?" the ferret shouted to her camerapeople.

"We got it, Francine!"

"Perfect. We'll use it when we launch the *Feathers Flying* version of *Furry Family Feud*. Okay. Hissletons and Montahughs? Take your places, please. We're live and on the air in one minute!"

"What?" said Theodosia. "Surely you can't expect us to play your silly quiz show under these circumstances."

"Thirty seconds to airtime!"

"Is this when I propose to Violet?" asked Phineas Fatt. Somewhere, he'd found a drumstick and was chomping on it. "Should I ask her to marry me now?"

"Nay!" cried Romaldo. "For I proposed to her first!"

"And I already said yes to Romaldo!" shouted Violet. "He is my soul mate, my one true love."

"No!" sobbed Phineas. "I'm heartbroken. Who's going to fetch me my supper? Which, by the way, I'd like in, oh, five minutes…"

"And we're live!" shouted the ferret.

The elephants blared a brassy fanfare. The scoreboard's tracer lights blinked to life. A prerecorded audience's applause and cheers boomed out of giant speakers.

The ferret sneered and spoke directly into the camera while, behind her, the Montahughs and Hissletons were jeering, barking, booing, hooting, squawking, screeching, squealing, and screaming.

"Ladies and gentlemen," Francine shouted into the camera, "this should be the most ferocious family feud ever played! As you can see, the fur is already flying! Because it's the feud to end all feuds! The Hissletons versus the Montahughs. This is gonna be some fight, right, Superintendent Bob?"

Bob the bear slumped into the frame and shrugged.

"I don't know, Francine," he said. "I mean, what's with all the fussing and fighting, anyhow? What the world needs now is—"

Francine tried to nudge him out of the frame. It didn't work. He was a bear. She was a ferret.

"Bob," she said, trying her best to spin the story back to action-packed conflict, "you know as well as I that these two families came to play. They're going to leave it all on the field. Fur, whiskers, broken claws, maybe a tooth or two. We might even see a few piles of poop in that field, because, you know, doggs..."

Oscar ran over to Molly.

"Our plan didn't work," he told her. "We have

to do something. Our families' feud is live and on TV!"

Molly sighed. "If only my grandmother and your grandfather could remember how they felt when they were Romaldo and Violet's age and fell in love with each other."

Oscar's eyes widened. "Maybe they can!"

Molly smiled. "And maybe we can help them do it!"

Chapter 59

We're gonna need Momsy!" Molly told Oscar, while their two families continued clashing and quarreling on the set of the quiz show and in front of an audience of millions.

"Momsy's still at the dam!" said Oscar. "She and the beavers were talking about the meaning of life. I'll run and fetch her."

"Because you're the fastest runner on your tennis ball team!"

"Yeah. What're you going to do?"

"Sing! That song by Katt Sneezins. You know, 'I Love My Dogg.'"

Oscar blushed. "No, I did not know that, but I am honored, I guess. Even though you just used the L word."

"Oscar, I don't love you."

Oscar looked hurt. "Oh. Okay. Never mind then..."

"I mean I am quite fond of you. You are my favorite dogg. But 'I Love My Dogg' is the title of the song that used to be my grandma and your grandpa's favorite. Remember?"

"Right! Back when they were acting even goofier than Romaldo and Violet. Back when they were young and in love and smooching on the Giant Stones and Momsy was going to marry them."

Molly nodded. "Maybe if I sing it, they'll remember."

"And if they don't," said Oscar, "Momsy can help them remember. I'll be back in a flash."

Oscar bolted for the woods.

Molly pushed her way through the bickering families and struggled to make it over to where

Francine the ferret was yammering into the camera.

"Well," said Francine, "we still haven't even asked our first quiz show question but already the contestants look ready to tear each other apart."

"But," said Bob, "let's hope that doesn't happen, Francine. You know, a friend of mine thinks the world would be a better place if we all just tried to get along. All I am saying is give peace a chance."

Francine looked stunned. "What the what? Have you flipped your lid?"

"Maybe," said Bob. "Or maybe my lady friend just helped me remember a kinder, gentler time. Sure she's a hippy-dippy, flakey-wakey, goofball throwback to the summer of love, but, you know, she has a point. I know she's made me reconsider some of my choices. Momsy has totally cast a spell on me, man. Again."

"So you're going to stop eating the salmon you snatch out of the river?"

Bob nodded. "I'm seriously considering it, Francine. I might become more of a nuts, berries, and tofu kind of bear. Then maybe the salmon could give me something even better than food. Maybe they could teach me how to swim. They're very good swimmers. They can even swim upstream, against the current. Come on. That's pretty cool…"

"Excuse me!" shouted Molly.

The ferret gave her a cheesy fake smile, because the cameras were still rolling. "Go join your family, sweetie pie. It's time to play the *Feud*. Our first category is Golden Oldies."

"Is it about songs?" asked Molly.

"No," said the ferret. "It's about ancient retrievers."

Molly bulldozed ahead (a trick she learned from the rhinos). "Because I know a song that the two golden oldies on both teams are gonna love. It's by Katt Sneezins and it's called 'I Love My Dogg.'"

"That's sweet, dearie, but—"

Molly took a step forward. All the cameras pushed in for a close-up.

"I love my dogg
Oh, yes, baby, I do.
And that dogg I love?
Baby, it's you…"

"Molly?" boomed her father. "We don't sing songs like that. They're against the rules. Those lyrics are lewd."

"No, they're not. Right, Grandmama?"

Theodosia Hissleton had been stunned silent. Grandpa Montahugh, too. Both their jaws were hanging open. When the other family members saw the looks on the two elderly faces, all the Hissletons and all the Montahughs quit their squabbling.

Everyone was silent, except for Molly, who kept humming the tune that seemed to make Grandma Theodosia and Grandpa Max remember happier days, back when they weren't so grouchy, grumpy, or lonely.

Chapter 60

Um, hello?" Francine shouted at all the Hissletons and Montahughs on the *Furry Family Feud* set.
(Phineas Fatt was napping in a sunny spot off camera, cuddling a kattnip pillow shaped like a cheese-
burger.) "You're supposed to be feuding here!"

"Shhh!" whispered Bob, planting a giant paw
on the ferret's tiny shoulder. "I think we're about
to have a moment, man." Bob put his other paw
over the camera lens. "That's it, folks. Show's over.
There's not going to be any more fussing, fum-
ing, or feuding. So turn off your TVs, walk next

door, and check in on your neighbor, man. See if they need anything. Put a little love in your heart. Peace out."

"We're clear!" shouted the camera operator. "The show is off the air." He touched his earpiece. "Permanently, they're telling me." He took off his headphones. "Come on, guys," he called to the rest of the crew, including the security elephants. "I have a friend who works on the *Love Dove* show. She says they're hiring."

"You ruined my big moment, Bob!" the ferret spat at the bear.

"Yeah, well, somebody had to do it. Before you ruined theirs." Bob gestured to Theodosia and Max. "Come on, Francine. Chill. There's some binturongs I want you to meet. Their pee smells like popcorn..."

Bob escorted the ferret off into the woods.

When they were gone, when it was just the katts and the doggs, Molly's grandmother spoke first. Her voice was softer and gentler than Molly had ever heard it. "Where did you learn that song, Molly dear?"

Molly smiled. "At your house, Grandmama. Remember? When I was little? You used to let me listen to your old records down in the basement."

Now Molly's grandmother grinned. "And you used to pretend you were singing along, clutching your fur brush as if it were a microphone."

Oscar's grandfather dabbed at a damp eye with the tip of his tail. "That Katt Sneezins was a good singer. And he wasn't even a katt."

"He was an otter!" laughed Molly's grandmother. "Remember, Max?"

Oscar's grandfather nodded. "But he was so cool and silky smooth, everybody called him Katt…"

And then they both said the exact same thing at the exact same time: "I'm sorry for those things I said that day."

Oscar came racing onto the set, panting. "Did I miss anything? Huh? Huh?"

"You sure did, Oscar," said his grandpa Max, pleasantly. "And you would've dug it, man."

Oscar gawped. "Hello, sir. Pleasure to meet you. I'm Oscar. What have you done with my grandfather?"

"Oh, I'm still me, Oscar," his grandfather said with a laugh. "In fact, I feel more like me than I have in a long, long time."

"Me, too," said Molly's grandmother. She held out her paws. Grandpa Max stepped forward and took them in his.

"Groovy." Momsy casually strolled in. "Guess you two didn't really need me," she said to Oscar and Molly. "Because, after all, you had each other."

Epilogue

Since Momsy, the polar bear, was still a licensed wedding officiant, the Hissletons and Montahughs asked her to preside over a double ceremony back at the rustic and spectacular welcome center in the Western Frontier Park.

Oscar and Molly were able to get the employee discount on the hall because they were back to doing shows, three times a week, after school. They needed to do that many shows because a lot of animals wanted to vacation together again, inspired by Max and Theodosia's love story.

As one raccoon put it, "Hey, if those two old coots can kiss and make up, I can vacation with a badger and a bunch of grubworms."

"It's so good to have the park full again!" proclaimed the hawkowl. "Thank you, Molly and Oscar, for once again showing the world that we're better when we work and play together."

Theodosia and Max felt the same way.

"I'm glad we had a second chance," said Max.

"Me, too," said Theodosia.

Violet and Romaldo were married right after Theodosia and Max. Violet went on to become a veterinarian. Romaldo became a world-famous architect designing animal hospitals (with lots of framed poetry on the walls to soothe anxious patients).

At Violet and Romaldo's wedding reception, Bob and Momsy announced *their* engagement. Everybody said that was far out. Man.

As more and more creatures learned to live together in peace and harmony, the Eastern Wilderness Reserve joined the Western Frontier Park and stopped segregating its untamed forests and streams into zoned-off animal sections.

"Hey, everybody should be able to enjoy it all, man," Bob told a WBN reporter who wasn't Francine the ferret. (Francine was at a "Scheming Management Seminar" that the Weasel Broadcasting Network suggested she take if she wanted to keep her job.) After his interview, Bob personally ripped down every single one of the *no trespassing* signs. He asked a binturong bear cat to join him. Because Bob loved the smell of popcorn.

And, on a spectacular late-summer evening, Oscar and Molly were crowned king and queen of the first-ever All Animals Ball at the Western Frontier Park (which wasn't canceled after all).

"Uh-oh," said Molly as they sat on their thrones, watching the dancers.

"What?" said Oscar. "What's wrong?"

"Nothing. Only we might need to ask Momsy to come back and perform another wedding."

"Really? How come?"

"Check it out. Phineas Fatt is dancing with your sister."

About the Authors

For his prodigious imagination and championship of literacy in America, **James Patterson** was awarded the 2019 National Humanities Medal, and he has also received the Literarian Award for Outstanding Service to the American Literary Community from the National Book Foundation. He holds the Guinness World Record for the most #1 *New York Times* bestsellers, including *Max Einstein, Middle School, I Funny,* and *Jacky Ha-Ha,* and his books have sold more than 400 million copies worldwide. A tireless champion of the power of books and reading, Patterson created a children's book imprint, JIMMY Patterson, whose mission is simple: "We want every kid who finishes a JIMMY Book to say, 'PLEASE GIVE ME ANOTHER BOOK.'" He has donated more than three million books to students and soldiers and funds more than four hundred Teacher and Writer Education Scholarships at twenty-one colleges and universities. He also supports 40,000 school libraries and has donated millions of dollars to independent bookstores. Patterson invests proceeds from the sales of JIMMY Patterson Books in pro-reading initiatives.

Chris Grabenstein is a *New York Times* bestselling author who has collaborated with James Patterson on the I Funny, Jacky Ha-Ha, Treasure Hunters, and House of Robots series, as well as *Word of Mouse, Katt vs. Dogg, Pottymouth and Stoopid, Laugh Out Loud,* and *Daniel X: Armageddon.* He lives in New York City.

Anuki López is an illustrator who has been drawing ever since she can remember—notebooks and pencils were her favorite childhood toys and she has never outgrown them! When Anuki is not drawing, she spends time with her lovely dog, Tanuki, who served as her drawing inspiration for *Katt vs. Dogg.* She lives in Seville, Spain.